I0744959

BY JAMIE EDMUNDSON

ME THREE
Og-Grim-Dog: The Three-Headed Ogre
Og-Grim-Dog and The Dark Lord
Og-Grim-Dog and The War of The Dead
Og-Grim-Dog: Ogre's End Game

THE WEAPON TAKERS SAGA
TORIC'S DAGGER
BOLIVAR'S SWORD
THE JALAKH BOW
THE GIANTS' SPEAR

Og-Grim-Dog and The War of The Dead

JAMIE EDMUNDSON

Rarn Publishing

Og-Grim-Dog and the War of The Dead
Book 3 of Me Three
Copyright © 2020 by Jamie Edmundson.
All rights reserved.
First Edition: 2020

ISBN 978-1-912221-08-0

Author website jamieedmundson.com

Cover Artwork: Andrey Vasilchenko

For Thomas

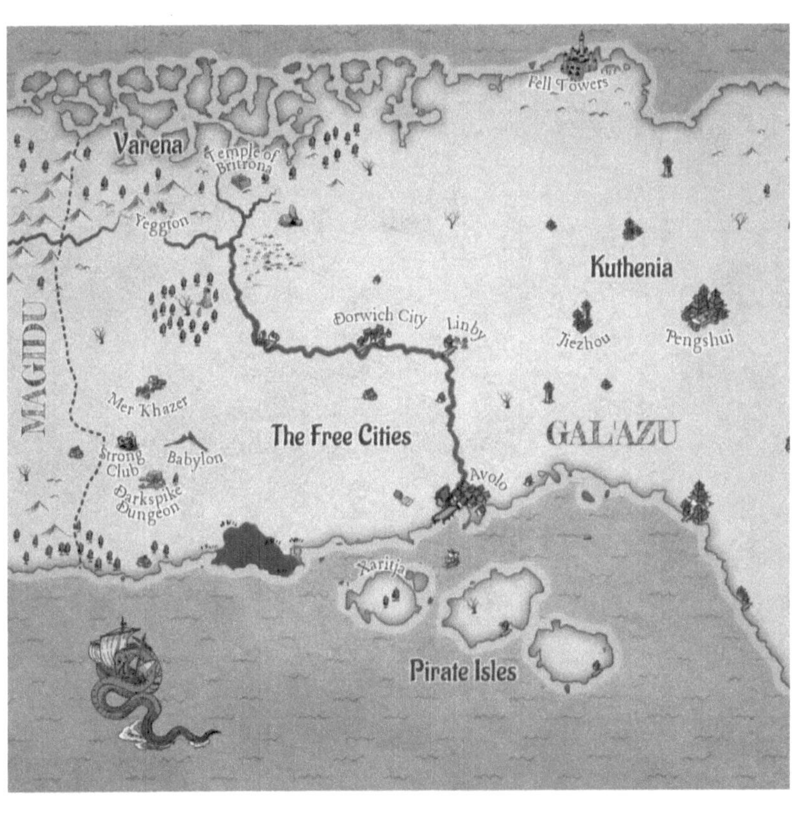

Fell Towers
Varena
Temple of Britrona
Yeggton
Kuthenia
MAGIDU
Dorwich City
Linby
Tiezhou
Pengshui
Mer Khazer
The Free Cities
GAL'AZU
Strong Club
Babylon
Darkspike Dungeon
Avolo
Xaritja
Pirate Isles

HOW WARS ARE STARTED

The Flayed Testicles had never been so full; the atmosphere never so fevered.

It had never been so full, because the inn had undergone a complete refurbishment. Tiered seating now faced a makeshift stage, where the Landlord's bar had once been. The old regulars of the Testicles now found themselves sharing the space with tourists from across Magidu. They looked on with bemused expressions as bar staff circulated, taking orders for interval drinks and offering a new type of beverage. Hard and cold, they called it iced cream. The regulars were used to their drinks warm and wet, and they muttered darkly amongst themselves at these new developments. But the truth of it was, they found themselves outnumbered.

It had never been so fevered, because tonight the infamous ogre of Gal'azu, Og-Grim-Dog, was to perform the third act of his life story. Many weeks had passed since the Recorder had left the inn to deliver his precious parchments to his publishing house. Since then, many copies of the work had been made, and the stories had been shared across the peaceable backwater that was Magidu. Public readings sprang up in every town. The wealthier citizens had purchased their own private copies, and tonight some of these were clutched in excitable, sweaty hands, whose owners hoped that they might get them signed by both the author and the subject of the tales.

But before either made their appearance, regulars and tourists alike were subjected to the warm-up act.

The man, who styled himself as a 'stand-up comedian', was sweating profusely as his act bombed. Part of the problem was that his brand of humour—observational comedy—was simply unknown in the land of Magidu. Give them some ribald wordplay, with a mother-in-law joke thrown in—possibly a piece about how stupid foreigners were—and the audience at the Testicles would have lapped it up. In Magidu, the audience muttered to one another, they liked comedy that was actually funny.

'So, I was thinking the other day, every other race has their 'thing', right? You know what I mean. Dwarves love gold, live in mountains.'

'Dwarves are short-arses!' someone in the audience offered, a comment that got the most laughs of the night so far.

The comedian persevered. 'Elves are a little up themselves, think they're better than everyone else.'

'Damn right!' several of those listening agreed.

'Goblins are ugly and nasty. Orcs, super-ugly, super-nasty. Trolls, really fucking ugly. Ogres—' he held his hands up and looked over his shoulder with a worried expression. 'Oh man, I'm not going there tonight!'

The comedian actually got some laughs for this. A light rekindled in his eyes—a sense of hope—that he might just win his audience around.

'But humans? I mean, what's *our* thing? Think about it. You get nice and nasty; greedy and selfless; rich and poor; clever and stupid; tall and short; fat and thin. It doesn't make any sense, right? How can all these other races have these really defining characteristics, and yet humanity is so diverse? So, I was thinking, we need to agree a set of characteristics for humans, and then we all have to stick to them.'

But the comedian didn't get any further. Confusion was quick to turn to anger, bewildered rumblings to indignant howls.

'Hey, lay off humans, you jerk!'

'Stick your characteristics where the sun don't shine!'

'Fuck you, then,' the warm-up act said under his breath and, in a final act of surrender, exited the stage.

Cheers followed him off, because his departure meant that the arrival of the main attraction was imminent.

First to appear was the Recorder. A warm round of applause greeted him as he made his way to the large desk that had been positioned just in front of the stage. He gave a wave to the audience, enjoying the attention. If they were interested in such details, the regulars at the Flayed Testicles would have noticed that the Recorder's clothes were new and much finer than those he had worn on his previous visit. Finally, he took his position on the chair at the desk. Laid out around him were the accoutrements of his profession: his parchment, ink and quill.

Then it was time for the grand entrance. Og-Grim-Dog, formerly known as the Landlord in these parts, came striding onto the stage. Cries of acclaim, whistles, and all the other excited noises associated with fame and celebrity greeted the three-headed ogre. His two arms rose in acknowledgement; two heads beamed with pleasure, while the third looked out over the hollering horde that filled their inn. An observant member of the audience might have noticed a suspicious, mistrustful look on this head's features.

'It's great to be here,' barked the first head into the noise. 'Back at ya, back at ya,' he added, pointing a finger at various figures in the audience, as if they were especially close friends.

The noise died down to an expectant hum.

'So—where were we?' asked the third head.

Chortles of laughter greeted this question, as if it was some great jest.

The Recorder cleared his throat, until the Flayed Testicles were ready to listen. 'After escaping from Fell Towers—that stronghold having fallen to the forces of Lilith and Samael—you and your friends returned to Mer Khazer. There, you killed Director Barclay of the Bureau of Dungeoneering, his position taken by Hassletoff the halfling. Hassletoff promptly made you an honorary member of the Bureau.'

'Ah, yes,' the ogre acknowledged. 'Though there was no time to go adventuring.'

'The War of The Dead?' prompted the Recorder.

'Indeed. We have given much thought about where to begin this story,' said the middle head. 'Most wars begin slowly, with baby steps. Then, before you know it, those baby steps have taken you past the point of no return. On our side, the first engagements of the war were not military, but diplomatic. We started out with three score members of the Bureau. The seizure of Discount Dungeon Supplies meant we had plenty of arms and armour. But we still needed an army. Delegations were sent out across our corner of Gal'azu, persuading the towns and cities that they needed to act against the threat from the Kuthenians and the new Dark Lord of Fell Towers. The wizard, Sandon Branderson, took up residence in the great city of Avolo, the jewel in the crown of this potential alliance. When his efforts resulted in Avolo's attachment to our cause, the League of the Free Cities became a reality. We finally had the resources to fund a standing army. It was perhaps at that moment that you could say the war began. Because it takes two armies to make a war.'

'And what of the infamous ogre, Og-Grim-Dog?' asked the Recorder. 'I mean no offence when I suggest that the delicate art of the diplomat was not one of your strengths.'

'You are both right and wrong. We would have been, at best, a spare part in an embassy sent to Avolo or Dorwich. But there were other participants in this war. Her Exalted Royal Majesty, Queen Krim, Sovereign and Despot of the Black Orcs of Darkspike Dungeon, Overlord of the Orc Nation. Our contribution was to bring the orcs of Gal'azu into the war. On our side.'

'The orcs? Pardon the expression, but what dog did they have in this fight?'

'There was an agreement that Queen Krim would gain her own kingdom in the south-west corner of Gal'azu, its borders respected by the League.'

'An orc kingdom?' the Recorder asked in an astonished voice. 'What of the villagers and farmers who had homes there?'

The ogre shrugged. 'These were all short-term decisions. The League needed Krim's soldiers. That's all they had the time to care about.'

'I see,' said the Recorder, scratching his quill along his first piece of parchment. 'And so, once you had an army, the fighting began?'

Three ogre heads nodded. 'It was decided that waiting for the enemy to come to us was poor strategy. Our greatest chance was to stir up the slaves of Kuthenia; to bring Princess Borte into that land—show the people that she lived. Encourage them to revolt against her uncle, the emperor. If we could march to Pengshui and place Borte on the throne, we would deliver a fatal blow to the enemy.'

'So, you have chosen to start your story in Kuthenia?'

'Aye. We'd been in Kuthenia for six months by this point. A turning-point in the war had come.'

HOW WARS END

A feast for crows had been left on the battlefield outside the city of Jiezhou. The army of the League of the Free Cities could claim another victory, since the Kuthenians had been forced off the field—retreating back to the east of their country. But no-one doubted they would be back, a fact that meant there was little celebration amongst the victors.

Og-Grim-Dog trudged through the churned-up grass towards the tents that had been erected behind the lines of the League's forces. If one wanted to be precise, one should in fact say that it was Grim who did the trudging, since the ogre's middle head controlled its two legs. The other heads, Og and Dog, had use of an arm each. They were the ones who had sliced and smashed their way through the ranks of the enemy, a force that the Kuthenians found difficult to stop.

Every step Grim took was a small victory over the physical and mental exhaustion that came after a battle. It was a state of exhaustion he had become familiar with over the last six months. When the adrenaline left the body, when the fear and battle madness was gone—all that borrowed energy dissipated—he was left an empty husk.

He headed for the army's central command tent. As he did after every battle, he looked anxiously to see if his friends had survived. First, he spotted Raya, the elf, and Hassletoff, the halfling, entering the tent ahead of him. Already inside were Assata, the barbarian, and Borte, the Kuthenian princess. Finally, the wizard, Sandon, entering with Caborna, the general of the Free Cities militia. Grim knew more soldiers had died today. But he narrowed his feelings to these five. When they made it back alive, he allowed himself a sense of relief. It was his way of coping with the horrendous losses he had witnessed over the last six months.

'That was brutal,' Assata admitted.

She commanded the division of freed slaves, who tended to be placed in harm's way in battle. They were the least likely to break—or, put another way, the most prepared to die, since they had the most at stake in this conflict.

Princess Borte gave the barbarian a comforting stroke on the arm. She led those Kuthenians who had turned against the Emperor to support his niece's claim to the throne. There were myriad reasons for making such a decision. Some were noble—but many were not—and Borte had to be careful how she handled her force.

General Caborna had command of the League's militia. He had the look of someone who had been born a soldier, long-limbed and disciplined in movement and speech, his dark hair on head and face only beginning to turn grey. His soldiers were men from the great cities such as Avolo and Dorwich, plus many more from the towns, villages and farms who owed allegiance to those cities. They were better equipped than the soldiers recruited in Kuthenia. But fighting on foreign soil, their commitment was less reliable, even though they were getting paid to do it.

Hassletoff's adventurers from the Bureau were a disparate group, rarely working as a whole unit. Clerics were needed to treat the injured. Magicians tended to work alone, on projects that Grim never fully understood. Occasionally he would witness the result of their work, when a bank of fog hid a unit of ambushers, or a sorcerer revealed the plans and disposition of the enemy. There was a core group, however, led by Raya. Their role was to intervene in the battle when and where most needed, often bolstering those units in danger. It was in this group that Og-Grim-Dog had found their place.

Finally, absent from the command tent, since her orcs were still deployed, was Queen Krim. Orcs didn't take well to disciplined formations or risking their lives. But once the battle had turned, it was their turn to be sent in and mop up any final resistance. Always keen to spill blood, they would chase the enemy for miles beyond the original battlefield.

In combination, these forces had been melded into a successful army. If the duties assigned to each weren't exactly fair, they were at least pragmatic, and as long as they kept winning, morale remained stable. Judging by the looks on the exhausted faces of those in charge, however, Grim had to wonder how much longer that would last.

'Congratulations on another victory,' said the general, his tone measured as always. 'However, I have to inform you of an order I have held off following until now. The League's forces are withdrawing from Kuthenia.'

Despite the understated way in which they were delivered, Caborna's words hit those in the room like a blow to the solar plexus.

'You can't do that!' Borte exploded. 'You'd be turning victory into defeat.'

'I'm sorry,' said Caborna. 'But the truth is, we've failed to reach Pengshui. That was our objective in Kuthenia, and it hasn't happened. All we're doing now is prolonging the bloodshed, with no end in sight. My men can't be expected to carry on like this forever.'

'What about our forces?' Assata demanded. 'You're leaving them here to be massacred?'

'No. They can withdraw west as well. I can't tell you what to do, but that would be my strong recommendation.'

'And what about those who have given their lives for this cause?' Assata continued. 'We must continue, for their sake.'

'Their deaths are no reason for more to die. I'm sorry, Assata,' Caborna repeated.

Assata and Borte turned to their friends, desperation clear on both faces, looking for support. Grim avoided making eye contact. For all he had come to love his friends, right now he felt that it was the general who was making the most sense.

'Why now?' Hassletoff asked the general, sticking up for his friends, even if he sounded a bit half-hearted. 'Why not continue a little longer? We might make a breakthrough.'

Caborna shook his head. 'We are just as likely to lose a battle, and then an orderly retreat becomes a dangerous rout.'

'Sandon?' Assata pleaded.

Sandon the wizard stood at Caborna's side. Part of the deal he had struck with the city of Avolo was that he would serve with the League's forces rather than the Bureau's. He gave Assata a sympathetic look. 'I've discussed the matter with General Caborna,' Sandon said. 'He has already ignored his orders and fought on longer than he should have. I think we need to retreat, now. Come up with a different plan.'

This was too much for the princess. Tears of frustration came, and she left the tent, one hand covering her face. Assata didn't leave, looking around the tent with a mad kind of fury.

'Remember this moment,' she said to them all, her eyes seeking theirs.

Grim was unable to resist any longer, looking into the anger that shone from his friend; and what was worse, the sense of betrayal that lay beneath it.

'When our enemies come to your homes and enslave the rest of Gal'azu; remember you could have chosen to fight on, and instead you decided to run.'

DIVISION

Og-Grim-Dog marched west with the army of the League of the Free Cities. Most of the soldiers were on foot, though there were enough horses to carry the injured and the supplies they needed. They used the roads of the Kuthenian Empire, that cut through the rich estates of the nobility of that land. Formerly farmed by slave labour; recently liberated and annexed by the League; now abandoned.

It was only ever going to be a miserable journey. They passed the settlements they had spilt blood to take, and the battle sites where they had won their victories, now giving them up without a fight. This was what defeat tasted like—the waste of life, the many acts of bravery and sacrifice erased. Worthless.

Sandon the wizard fell in with the ogre. He gave the three heads an anxious look.

'Are you angry with the decision?' he asked.

Grim shared a look with his brothers. 'Last year, Assata, Gurin and I got to Pengshui in less time than it took us to reach Jiezhou with an army.'

Gurin Fuckaxe, Grim mused. They could have done with his axe and penchant for violence in this war. But he had left last year, on a quest to rescue his dwarven friends. Something about having sold them to a travelling circus.

'And no-one got killed, either,' Og added to Grim's statement.

Even Dog, who was usually as enthusiastic as anyone about fighting, nodded in agreement. 'There must be another way.'

'I think so too,' said Sandon, his voice a mixture of relief and enthusiasm. 'If we had succeeded in taking the Empire away from Samael's grasp it would have been worth our efforts. But we have to admit that we've failed: Kuthenia is too big to take by force. Instead, we need to think about how to deal with the real enemy: Lilith and Samael. They are the threat, not a nation or a people.'

'And how do we do that?' Dog asked. 'Go back to Fell Towers and bash the succubus over the head with my mace?'

Sandon smiled. 'Unfortunately, it won't be so simple, Dog. That is the problem that has presented itself to us, and the truth is, we have done nothing to find a solution. There are two demons at large in Gal'azu, and I have no idea how to destroy them. An assassination attempt, even if it is carried out by the best the Bureau has to offer, will almost certainly lead to our deaths. And then there will be no-one left to stop them.'

Grim looked at his brothers a second time, a question in his eyes. They both gave him a silent nod of approval.

'Sandon, there is something we should perhaps have mentioned before now.'

The wizard raised an eyebrow but gave the ogre a silence to speak into.

'When we were working for the Dark Lord—the previous one—Lilith sent us on a mission to Varena. We visited the Oracle of Britrona and extracted from her the identities of individuals who she divined were a threat to the Dark Lord.'

'And?' Sandon asked, his voice sharper than usual.

'And then we proceeded to kill them. All of them. We can't help wondering if that was a mistake. Is it possible that some of those individuals might have had certain powers, that could have helped us?'

Sandon gave the idea some considerable thought, walking alongside the ogre in a contemplative silence. Finally, he replied. 'I think it would be a good idea to visit the Oracle, sooner rather than later.'

✧

The army continued its westward march, through the no-man's land where the reach of the Empire ended, into the land dominated by the great cities of the River Auster. As they approached the town of Linby, the sound of the river rippling by could be heard. Here it turned south, on its last leg before meeting the sea.

It was at this point that the League's army separated. General Caborna would follow the course of the river to Avolo, with a substantial number of Free City soldiers. In addition, some of the Kuthenians who had left their homeland behind had decided to make their new homes in the great seaport of Gal'azu.

It was not an easy parting. Assata and Borte had not forgiven the general for his decision and made a point of ignoring his departure. Sandon's farewells were genuine, but nonetheless the wizard had decided not to return to Avolo, his mind now on the Oracle to the north. Hassletoff and Caborna shared some vague sentiments about continuing to work together, but it was hard to escape the feeling that the League was breaking up.

Once they reached Dorwich City, Queen Krim of the Orc Nation disbanded her force, sending them back to the dungeons and other dark places of Gal'azu. The question of an Orc Kingdom remained unresolved, but Grim knew it hadn't gone away. Krim had been made a promise, and she wasn't going to forget that.

Another blow to the League followed. Deston was the reeve of Dorwich, and he had raised the second largest contingent in the Free Cities militia. Now his soldiers would be allowed home.

'I've fought with you the last six months,' he said to the small group from the Bureau outside the gates of his city, 'and I figure you deserve to know how things stand. I expect the Kuthenian army to come this way, sooner or later. I can predict their strategy: they'll head straight here, cut the League lands in two. When that happens, I'll be acting in the best interests of the people of this city. I'll not hesitate to bend the knee to the Emperor if it spares Dorwich a bloody siege.'

'You're switching sides?' Assata demanded, seemingly unable to accept the words, though they had been clear enough.

'I'll switch sides when the time comes,' Deston confirmed. 'Dorwich will survive, its people continue to prosper. Like I said, I owed you the truth.'

'Well,' said Hassletoff. 'I appreciate the honesty, even if the backbone's missing.'

Deston shrugged, unaffected by the insult—perhaps expecting it. 'When the Kuthenians are outside Mer Khazer you can prove how much more backbone you have, and see your town put to the sword. That's up to you.'

Despite the losses taken, the force that returned to Mer Khazer was larger than the one that had left. The majority of the freed slaves had followed Assata and Borte here, putting their faith in their liberators, as well as many Kuthenians with a personal loyalty to the princess. In the circumstances, it was an advantage to have such a force to help defend the town. But accommodation for the newcomers had to be speedily constructed, and the concerns of the existing townsfolk assuaged.

Such issues were the business of politics, and they dominated the thoughts of Hassletoff, Borte and Assata. For others, though—notably Sandon the wizard—there were other priorities to consider. Things came to a head when Raya called for a meeting at The Bruised Bollocks.

'We need to clear the air,' the elf began. 'Resolve our differences.'

But Raya was being too optimistic.

'All the things we need to get done,' Assata said after listening to Sandon, too quick to lose her temper these days, 'and you want to go on an adventure into Varena?'

'That's unfair,' said Sandon mildly. 'A visit to The Oracle may be the only way we learn how to defeat Lilith and Samael. That makes it the most important thing we can do right now.'

'Then go!' said the barbarian. 'Get your palms read, find out what she sees in her crystal ball. Meanwhile, some of us still have an Empire to defeat.'

Hence, later that day, a wizard, an elf and an ogre left Mer Khazer, and a barbarian, a halfling and a princess stayed behind.

PROPHECY

Ordinarily, a party travelling from Mer Khazer to Britrona would have to plan a rather roundabout journey, detouring past the most troublesome locations. Even then, the terrain would be difficult and not without dangers. With Raya's expertise, however, Og-Grim-Dog and his two friends were able to take the most direct route possible. It involved striking through the Deepwood, an old forest full of strange creatures. Last time they had travelled here, on their way to Deepwood Dungeon, Og-Grim-Dog had been attacked by a giant spider; while Sandon had faced a close call with the Queen of the Fairies.

This time, Raya promised that no such horrors would appear. How she could guarantee this, Grim had no idea. But Sandon trusted her implicitly, and as the hours turned into days, and their progress continued uninterrupted, Grim began to relax. Raya was able to navigate with a woodsman's confidence, finding one animal trail after another, building a path that kept them going in a northerly direction. Her skill with the bow also kept them supplied with enough fresh meat to satisfy a hungry ogre, which she supplemented with a surprising variety of edibles from her evening forages. Eventually, Grim noticed the Deepwood begin to thin out, until they finally left the forest behind.

'This means we're beyond the half-way point,' Raya informed, as they made camp in the open. 'Perhaps that calls for a celebration,' she added, pulling a bag of wine from her sack.

It was the first time in a while they had slept without trees towering above them, branches creaking in the wind and the unnerving nocturnal sounds of the forest to disturb them. Grim awoke better rested as a result.

The next part of the journey saw them traversing through an un-named, no-man's land of rocky plains. It was here that Dog caught the scent of trolls.

'They're up ahead,' he warned, pointing towards an outcrop of rock in the distance. 'Probably waiting to ambush us.'

'Then let's change course,' said Sandon, gesturing to the north-east.

'They won't give up now they have our scent,' said Og in a resigned voice.

Sure enough, once the trolls realised that their quarry were detouring around their hiding place, they left the outcrop, cutting towards them.

'Three of them,' said Grim.

They came in the unhurried way of trolls, but their long, loping strides were bringing them closer, nevertheless.

Grim and his friends picked up their speed, moving fast enough to get ahead of them. The trolls responded, trotting after them, spreading out slightly—a standard troll manoeuvre before an attack. Raya loosed an arrow. The lead troll was unable to move out of the way and took the missile in the shoulder.

'He'll be hurt,' mused Og, 'but it won't stop him.'

The trolls continued to follow them, but they backed off a little now, wary of the elf's bow. Trolls were patient hunters. Clearly, these three still fancied their chances, perhaps thinking a night-time attack would give them an advantage.

'River up ahead,' said Raya, her ears the first to pick up the sound of rushing water. 'A tributary of the Auster. I wonder if they're driving us into a trap?'

'Could be,' said Grim.

'Keep going,' said Sandon. As the roar of the river got louder, the wizard began to run. 'Come, quick!' he shouted.

Grim did his best to run after him, wary of tripping and falling. Next to him, Raya was light on her feet, turning around and releasing another arrow to dissuade the trolls from following too fast.

Grim stopped when he reached Sandon, breathing hard. It was a steep drop down to the river, full of boulders and rocks. More than enough obstacles to slow his movement down to a crawl and allow the trolls to attack. Mercifully, it appeared that Sandon had already begun to murmur a spell. The wizard's head swivelled around.

'I learned this—'

'Please, Sandon,' said Og. 'Tell us afterwards.'

'Right.'

The wizard completed his spell. Grim's eyes nearly popped out of his head as he watched Sandon step off the edge of a boulder and begin walking on air.

'Follow where I tread,' Sandon said to Grim and Raya. 'Come on, it's perfectly safe.'

Grim was not about to break an ankle by stepping into thin air.

Raya followed behind the wizard, the pair of them moving over the roiling water below.

'I can't do that,' said Grim, panic coursing through his body at the strange sight. 'I really don't think it will take my weight.'

'They're coming,' Dog warned.

'Come on, Grim,' Og said encouragingly. 'You can do it.'

Grim knew he had to try. He reached a foot out into space, fully expecting to tumble off the edge of the boulder. His foot came down on a smooth surface. It felt strong enough, even if it was invisible. Committing now, Grim put all his weight on his front foot and moved forwards. Somehow, he wasn't falling. He decided not to think about it anymore and followed Sandon and Raya.

The wizard and elf soon reached the other side of the river. They waved for Grim to continue. He smelled the trolls coming behind him and kept going. Raya held her hand out encouragingly and when they got within range, she grabbed Og's hand and helped them onto the rocky riverbank. Grim stood still for a while, his legs shaking, before he turned around to look at the opposite bank.

The three trolls were staring at them, their small black eyes showing little emotion—though surely, they must be frustrated at losing their quarry a second time. For, now that Grim had the luxury of being able to study them carefully, he knew he was looking at the same three brothers they had encountered in Varena last year.

'Better luck next time!' Grim shouted across the noise of the water, before he and his companions left the trolls and the river behind, and continued on their journey.

✳

Even though Britrona was located in the wilds of Varena, accounts of the Oracle's prophetic powers had spread far and wide—across Gal'azu and beyond—so that many well-worn tracks to the town wound their way over hill and dale. Og-Grim-Dog and their two companions soon found one and joined the steady stream of travellers on their way to or from the Temple.

As they entered the town, Grim could see that little had changed since their visit last year. Apart from the fact that it catered for so many tourists, Britrona was an ordinary looking town. It was the Temple that was of interest, and they wasted no time in heading straight there.

Unfortunately, as they approached the home of the Oracle, it appeared that some changes had been made at the Temple. In particular, security seemed much tighter, and Grim couldn't help but think that this might be down to Og-Grim-Dog's previous visit. Threatening to kill the Oracle unless she coughed up her secrets had worked at the time; but might not have been the best approach to guarantee a long-term working relationship.

Sure enough, as they approached the entrance to the Temple, frenetic activity suggested that not only had they been seen, but that the arrival of a three-headed ogre triggered an emergency response. Soldiers, dressed in a basic woad dyed uniform over leather armour and armed with shield and spear, began to file out of the building. One of their number began issuing orders, organising them into a line, shields overlapping and spears pointing ahead.

'Sorry,' said Grim. 'I think this is because of us.'

'Let me deal with this,' said Sandon. 'It was while enrolled in the Sect of the Nameless Purveyors of Pandemonium that I learned how to influence the minds of lesser mortals. It's not a skill I enjoy using, but sometimes the situation demands it.'

He held out his staff, the blue orb of Relandra emitting a pale light as it conducted his magic.

'We need to see the Oracle,' he said to the leader of the Temple's soldiers.

'You need to see the Oracle,' the man agreed.

'Put down your weapons. We are not a threat.'

'Put down your weapons,' the man ordered his soldiers. 'They are not a threat.'

The soldiers shared some puzzled looks but complied with their orders.

'Come,' said the man, gesturing at Sandon and his friends. 'I will take you to see the Oracle.'

It was hardly surprising that the meeting with the Oracle was a difficult one. She had an aura about her, a certain star quality that lifted her above mortals—even royalty like Princess Borte—who still had to dwell in the material world. The Oracle dwelt in a different world—a hallowed world of mystery—and she clearly wasn't used to not getting her own way. Not only had Og-Grim-Dog behaved very badly towards her when they had first met; he and his friends had now beguiled their way past the defence force she had clearly put a lot of effort and expense into ensuring it didn't happen again.

But still, in the end, she listened to what they had to say. Sat on a throne before them in her private rooms, dressed in a white chiton with her loose red hair flowing beyond her shoulders, it was like asking a favour of a resentful goddess.

'So, let me get this right,' she said, when she heard what they had to say, 'you are not looking for *forgiveness* for your crimes? You want to somehow *undo* the heinous murders you committed? Wouldn't life be so much easier if we could just erase every mistake we make? Why, there would be no need to think about the consequences of our actions at all. We could do as we please, like heedless, senseless children.'

Grim got the feeling that there was a sarcastic kind of criticism to her words, but it was lost on some people. Dog nodded in agreement with the Oracle, and when she was done, replied 'Yes, that would be delightful.'

'The thing is,' said Sandon, 'Gal'azu is under a very great threat. If we were doing this just to make Og-Grim-Dog feel better, then we would fully deserve your scorn. But there are two demons at large in our land. This ogre is just one of many creatures who fell under their spell. A mindless puppet in their plans.'

'Bit rude,' Og said under his breath.

'I fear that if we don't act now, our world will soon be lost.'

The Oracle pursed her lips. 'Very well,' she relented. The Oracle closed her eyes and a silence descended on the room. No doubt it was just his imagination, but Grim felt like the small space they inhabited somehow shifted away from their plane of existence and connected with another.

The Oracle shook her head, scrunching her face as if in pain, and then emitted a cry of fear. 'A darkness sweeps the land,' she said, her voice much changed, deeper and slower in speech, as if it were no longer her voice at all. She moaned. Her eyes remained closed as she spoke. 'The dead are restless. Hungry. The living are scattered. Lost. It is the end times.' She gasped for air as if she had been drowning and her eyes flashed open. The Oracle looked around her until she had focused on her surroundings. She looked at Og-Grim-Dog and Sandon and Raya, who waited patiently for her news. 'The future is even worse than you thought,' she said at last. 'A terrible deed has been done. Perhaps it is possible to change what I have seen,' she said doubtfully. 'Xaritja, third island of the Pirate Isles, has a smaller island off its coast. Uninhabited, yet guarded. There you will find portals that may take you to another place or time. It is the only chance you have of saving Gal'azu.'

DOWN THE AUSTER

The best form of transport to the south coast of Gal'azu from Varena was via the Auster. They negotiated the purchase of two solid-looking canoes that would take them down the fast-flowing upper course of the river. When they had left Mer Khazer for the north, the plan had been to return with whatever information they had gleaned from the Oracle and share it with their friends in the Bureau. But the seer's vision had emphasized the urgency of their quest. A reunion would have to wait.

Og and Dog faced a unique challenge in establishing the co-ordination required to paddle a canoe. Grim found himself in the middle of a lot of shouting. He resisted the urge to join in or give his own advice. It was better to let his brothers sort it out between them. Instead, Grim switched off, going to a quiet place. It was a technique he had developed as a young ogre, when the stress of being stuck between two unruly juveniles got too much. He focused instead on the clear water of the Auster; on the branches of the trees leaning over the river to catch the sun. He focused on the waterfowl—leading their own lives; uninterested in the quarrelling three-headed ogre in the canoe; oblivious of the wars of men; or the dark prophecies of oracles.

Once his brothers got the hang of paddling, they began to make good time, their powerful arms pulling their craft through the water. Sandon and Raya, in the other canoe, began to find it hard to keep up. Although the river was fast and strong at this point, rapids and sharp falls meant they had to take care, taking the vessels out of the water at certain points. At these times Og and Dog grabbed a canoe each and half-carried, half-dragged them to the next stretch. As the Auster matured, changing its course for the east, its pace slowed—but the obstacles disappeared, allowing them a gentler and easier passage.

After several days of travel, they reached Dorwich City. Here, the river was busy with craft and it made sense for them to sell their canoes and book passage on a barge to Avolo. Remembering the reeve's words when they were last here some two weeks ago, they were keen to ask at the docks about the news from Kuthenia. It was surprisingly good. There had been no signs of the Kuthenian military leaving the Empire and encroaching on the territory of the League. The only rumour that had come from the east was a sickness sweeping that land, which perhaps explained the lack of activity.

'No army hereabouts means that Mer Khazer is safe for the time being,' Raya commented.

'Is it possible the Oracle's vision was wrong?' Og suggested. 'After all, it hardly feels like the end of days here,' he said, gesturing at the city docks, that were just as busy as usual.

'I'd rather operate as if it were true and be pleasantly surprised if it turns out to be false,' said Sandon.

The barges left Dorwich City, carrying timber, metal, cloth and many other goods along the Auster. The stop in Linby was of particular interest to Grim and his friends. Its proximity to the Empire meant that the town was most likely to have news of an invasion force. But here too, the only talk was of the sickness.

'Sends people mad, so they say,' said one of the dockers on Linby's wharf. 'Bite and scratch like animals. We had some fugitives from the Empire come in the other day, one of the women had been chewed on by a deranged Kuthenian. She came down with a fever and didn't linger long with it.'

'She died?' Sandon asked.

'Aye.'

'Can you take us to see her compatriots?' the wizard asked, offering the man a silver coin. 'We're setting off soon: you'd have to take us now.'

✳

Five slaves had arrived in Linby three days ago, taking an opportunity to escape their farmstead. Four remained. All were young adults, strong enough and brave enough to come into a foreign land. They had plans to go to Dorwich City, maybe carry on as far as Mer Khazer. For now, though, they seemed too exhausted to move. With no home, they sat in a street in Linby, dependent on the charity of the townsfolk for food. They were grateful for the money Sandon gave them; willing to share their story.

'The sick came to our farm,' one of the two women explained, 'attacking the animals and people alike. In the chaos we got away, decided to leave Kuthenia for good.'

'But your friend was bitten?' Raya asked.

'My sister, Nevaeh,' said one of the men. 'She was bit at the farm. She just got sicker and sicker.'

'How did she die?' Sandon asked.

Grim couldn't miss the sudden tension, the quick looks that passed between the group.

'She just got weaker and weaker, until she passed,' said the woman.

'And she's buried here, in town?' Sandon asked.

'We buried my sister ourselves, yesterday. Took her body out into the wild.'

Back on the barge, heading south for Avolo, Grim and his friends tried to make sense of what they had heard.

'They were lying about the way the girl died,' said Raya.

Grim nodded in agreement. 'What were they trying to hide?'

'That they killed her themselves,' said Sandon. 'They were scared of getting into trouble for it—of falling foul of the town authorities.'

'What drove them to do that?' Raya wondered.

'She was bitten,' said Og. 'Had the sickness. Maybe that left them no choice, in the end.'

'The dead are restless. Hungry,' said Sandon, recalling the words of the Oracle. 'The living are scattered. Lost.'

✵

The journey south from Linby to Avolo was a straightforward one. The river was thick with craft on this stretch, perhaps the busiest trading route in all of Gal'azu.

While the bargemen began unloading their goods onto the docks, built where the river met the sea, Og-Grim-Dog, Sandon and Raya headed for the nearest city gate. It allowed entry through the great stone walls of the city. While those with goods to bring in had to wait in a toll queue, there was a separate entrance for pedestrians.

At first, the city guards looked set to deny Og-Grim-Dog entry, but one of their number hailed them in a friendly manner. It turned out he had fought in Kuthenia with them, and his colleagues relaxed and nodded. It seemed they had heard of the ogre who had fought with their compatriots abroad, and the three of them were quickly waved through.

Sandon had resided in Avolo for months and he began to lead them through the maze of streets with confidence. They were teeming with humans and other races, unlike anywhere else Grim had ever been—even Pengshui, the great capital of Kuthenia. For while Pengshui occupied the same sized space, it had a sense of planning and order. Avolo, on the other hand, was a chaotic jumble of dwellings and commercial buildings. Most foreign ships used Avolo as their port in Gal'azu, dropping off passengers from other continents daily. And while some of these newcomers chose to strike out into the great realm beyond the city walls, many decided to make their home here, where others of their folk could provide a warm welcome and a helping hand.

'City hasn't changed much since we were last here,' said Dog, looking around. 'I wonder if there'll be time for a quick visit to The Smashed Marbles?'

'I don't recall us ever visiting Avolo before,' said Og.

Sandon's connections meant that they were quickly able to gain access to the man the wizard thought might help them. Caborna owned a house in the centre of the city. Inside, it was austere by human standards. The general took them to his kitchen and gave them bread, cheese and ham, washed down with the white wine that was produced on the south coast of Gal'azu.

'This is delicious,' Raya enthused, draining her third cup.

'Well, here,' said Caborna, grabbing a second barrel. 'Please, take this with you on your travels.'

The elf's eyes lit up and she gave it a little pat. 'Thank you. That's enough for me, but what about these guys?'

Raya laughed at her own joke—for longer, and more hysterically, than was entirely comfortable.

'I can charter you a private vessel to Toyer, the island you speak of that sits off Xaritja,' Caborna told them. 'The voyage is less dangerous than you might think, since it's not a route commonly sailed, and you'll stay close enough to our navy's sphere of influence. It's to the south and east that the pirates of the Isles like to operate, where they can intercept the trading vessels that carry goods worth stealing. Still, it's the island itself that I should warn you about.'

'The Oracle spoke of it a little,' said Sandon. '"Uninhabited, yet guarded," were her words.'

'The island has a guardian, so it's said,' Caborna confirmed. 'Who or what they are guarding, and from what peril, is more open to interpretation.'

'The portals?' Grim prompted.

'Aye, there are plenty of stories about the portals. You can imagine the myriad reasons why someone might wish to travel to some other place or time. All I can say for sure is, virtually none who do so ever return to tell the tale themselves.'

THE GUARDIAN OF THE PORTALS

The Avoluese cog bobbed along on the ocean as Og-Grim-Dog inhaled the salty air. It wasn't a big vessel, but for all Grim's anxiety about trusting his life to this ship, it felt sturdy enough underfoot. Still, the thought that should he and his brothers end up in the Great Wet, they would certainly drown, never fully disappeared.

Caborna had been right. Every other vessel leaving Avolo had set course for the east, making for the Kuthenian Empire or the great continents that lay in that direction. Their little cog was the sole exception. The only reason to head west was either for the quiet and peaceable realm of Magidu, or the lightly populated island of Xaritja. Beyond those two destinations, most sailors believed there was nothing, save for giant sea serpents that would eat a craft such as this in one mouthful.

'That is Toyer,' said the ship's captain, pointing out a slight bump on the horizon.

He was a tight-lipped fellow who seemed keen to get them to their destination and be off again. He knew what he was about though, and it wasn't long after spotting the island that they were nearing the empty beach. The island of Toyer looked mostly flat, consisting of sand and rock and not much else; though Grim could discern a rocky ridge in the centre of the island, dotted with trees and other greenery.

There were no docks for the cog to moor onto, and so it was a rather undignified clamber over the side and into the waves that was required.

'I'll be back for you in a week,' the captain promised them, calling down from the side of his craft.

'And on this day every week thereafter,' Sandon reminded him.

'Aye,' the captain acknowledged. He then began shouting commands at his crew, manoeuvring his craft back out to sea.

Grim began to slog his way through the water that lapped back and forth, his feet sinking into the wet sand beneath. Sandon and Raya came with him, the wizard cursing as he tried to keep his robes out of the water. Somehow, the elf made the process of walking to shore look effortless, and she was first to reach the dry sand. She continued up the beach, heading for a cluster of rocks that would afford her a better view of the island.

'Oh, this is awful,' Grim said as he finally emerged from the water, the dry sand of the beach sticking to his wet feet.

'Quit complaining,' said Dog, 'and follow that elf.'

'I'm not sure where we're supposed to go,' Raya said as Grim took up position next to her.

Indeed, a glance around what they could see of the island from here revealed no buildings—no signs of human habitation. Sandy soil and bare rock covered much of the area around them, while the land rose steadily to the ridge in the distance, no paths visible that might help them reach it. It was impossible to say what was on the other side.

'Looks like a hard place to live off,' said Grim. He was beginning to think that this might turn out to be a very long week they were about to endure, before the cog returned. 'It's no wonder no-one's tried to make their home here.'

'Or if they did try, they gave up,' Dog added.

'Well?' Sandon asked as he joined them.

'Without sounding overly negative,' said Og, 'our task feels a little vague. No-one has told us what these portals might look like, or where they are located. Are we supposed to search every inch of this island until we find something?' He waved his hand around at the scene before them. 'That may take a while.'

'Why don't you wait here, while I explore?' Raya suggested pleasantly. 'It's the kind of thing I'm good at.'

Grim wasn't about to argue. He'd learned that despite appearances, Raya was a formidable figure, well able to look after herself.

As if to emphasise his thoughts, the elf shrugged her pack from her shoulders, took out her bow and strung it. 'Just in case,' she said, before turning to Dog. 'And remember,' she added, gesturing at the pack. 'That wine barrel is mine.'

It wasn't so bad, sitting on a rock on a deserted island. First, they watched the cog disappear into the distance. Then Sandon tried to dry out his robes, while Grim tried to get his brothers to remove the sand from between his toes. But all in all, it was a peaceful place, and Grim had enjoyed little of that in recent months. The war in Kuthenia had been an unpleasant experience—it almost made an ogre crave his dungeon cavern, or his house in the swamp.

Perhaps it was this brief moment of tranquillity, or perhaps the fact that keeping lookout wasn't really a strength of either the ogre or the wizard—but neither heard the elf reappear until she was in front of them. Raya had a little smile on her face.

'Hello,' she said.

'Well?' Dog asked. 'Any news?'

'May I introduce Elsie,' said Raya, her hand reaching near her shoulder.

'What in Gehenna?' Dog let out.

Grim gave a start. For sitting on Raya's shoulder, unnoticed until now, was a fairy. It flew off the elf's shoulder, tiny wings fluttering, and then landed on her hand. Grim could see that this fairy was a brunette, wearing clothes the colour of autumn.

'Elsie is the guardian of this island,' Raya informed them. 'This is Sandon and Og-Grim-Dog.'

'A f-fairy?' Sandon stuttered. 'I had a bad experience with a fairy. Remember when the Queen of the Fairies tried to abduct me in the Deepwood?'

Elsie gave Sandon a look that was part bemusement, part derision. 'The Queen of the Fairies?' she repeated.

Given her size, Grim had been expecting the fairy to have a child-like voice, but instead it had a rich, deep timbre, though still feminine.

'Yes, well,' said Raya quickly. 'We haven't time to go on about that. We have come looking for a portal.'

'I am the guardian of the portals on this island,' said the fairy. 'I decide whether you can go where or when you wish. And I always exact a price—one that most cannot afford.'

'Who made you the guardian?' Og asked. 'And where do the portals come from?'

Grim sometimes wished his brother would rein it in a bit when they met a new person.

'Interesting questions,' said Elsie, 'though ones I'm not about to answer.'

'Well,' said Grim, 'we wish to travel in both space and time. We need to get to Varena, last year, to stop a series of assassinations.'

'And who carried out these killings?'

'We did.'

'He means we,' Dog clarified, gesturing to himself and his two brothers. 'Not them,' he added, pointing at Raya and Sandon.

'I see,' Elsie said. 'A quest inspired by regret?'

'Partly,' said Grim. 'But also, we think we may have killed some people we really shouldn't have. People who might have saved the world—or at least saved Gal'azu.'

Elsie gave a tiny shrug. 'I often hear talk of saving the world. The world can be turned in various directions, often by an apparently insignificant action. It is hard to predict, standing from one point in time and looking ahead to another, whether the results will be good or bad. Usually, of course, they are a mixture: good for some and bad for others. What gives you the right to change the course of history?'

'Two things,' said Sandon, recovering from his initial shock. 'An incubus and a succubus. The first, concealed in the court at Pengshui, now controls the Empire. The second has become the new Dark Lord of Fell Towers. The situation in Gal'azu has become critical. If we do nothing, it will be a land ruled by demons. I cannot say for sure what will happen should we change the course of history. But I judge it is worth the risk.'

Elsie gave Sandon a look, as if reappraising the wizard. 'Very well. Then it comes to the question of payment. I collect magic infused objects. One object, of sufficient power, in exchange for the use of a portal.'

Heads, naturally enough, turned to Sandon. 'Ah, well. I must admit to not being overburdened with magical objects, unfortunately. I have but two: my Ring of Curse-Breaking and the Staff of Relandra. I came into possession of the staff more recently: so one could argue, easy come, easy go.'

'I also think the ring made a noticeable difference to your magic,' said Og.

'You think? I hadn't really noticed myself, but if you say so…'

'There is my Amulet of Hiding, also,' said Raya, patting her pack.

'Though that has come in handy more than once,' said Grim quickly.

'Most of those seeking a portal do not arrive with a magic object already in their possession,' said Elsie. 'They immediately go off to find one. That option is always open to you.'

'I wonder how many return,' said Raya.

The fairy gave the elf a sly smile.

'We don't have time for that,' said Sandon, coming to a decision. 'The staff it is.' He held it out. 'Erm, how do you want me to—'

'Leave it on the ground,' Elsie said. 'Now. The appropriate portal is not far from here. Raya, that way, if you please.'

The fairy led the elf across the island, the ogre and wizard following behind. In only a short while they came to a beach, wide and sandy just like the one they had first arrived on. The sound of the waves and the emptiness all around them gave it an otherworldly atmosphere.

'Now then,' said Elsie, looking about the shore. 'Ah, that rock over there, Raya, do you see it?'

They walked over to a small, unremarkable looking rock lying on the sand.

'Erm. You've taken us to see a rock?' asked Dog.

'I can make the portals look like anything I wish. I choose to make them blend in. A rock, a blade of grass. Even a grain of sand. Though those ones are quite hard to keep track of. Here, is this better?'

Before their eyes, the rock changed. In its place was a wooden door, smooth and slim, with a handle fashioned from metal.

Unconnected to any kind of frame or wall, the door nonetheless stood straight and true.

'Reminds me of the time we mistakenly went through that door to Gehenna,' said Dog with a bark of laughter. 'Took us nearly three weeks to get out again, remember? I stopped drinking absinthe after that.'

Grim paced around to the other side of the door. There *was* no other side. Just his friends, a fairy, and behind them the footprints they had made in the sand.

Tempted to walk back through the door that wasn't there, instead Grim elected to retrace his steps around it. As he drew level with the thin edge, it reappeared.

'Well, well,' he muttered.

'No lock on it,' said Og.

Grim twisted the metal handle and pulled. The door swung towards him smoothly. Through the door, his senses told him, were trees and hills and valleys, fast flowing streams and lakes and fjords, dark soil and high mountain air. 'It is Varena,' he said, for some reason as sure of the statement as if he had declared an egg to be an egg.

THE UNKILLING OF KARLENS STONE

Og-Grim-Dog squeezed their way through the door on Toyer Island into Varena. They found themselves in a remote spot on the northern coast. From their position on a rocky cliff, Grim could look down on the Northern Sea. A few miles farther north, a mountainous island rose out of the waves, shrouded in a mist that hid the peaks from view.

Turning around, he witnessed the strange sight of Sandon the wizard walking through the door. Behind him, framed by the doorway, was the golden sand of the island and the blue sky of the Pirate Isles. And yet, beyond the confines of the doorway, Grim could see the angular grey peaks of Varenian mountains, and a thick forest of spruce.

Last to come through was Raya. She said a farewell to Elsie, who fluttered out of sight.

'She says this doorway will remain open.'

'For how long?' Sandon asked.

'Until we come back through.'

'What if we never do?' asked Og.

Raya shrugged. 'I don't know. Elsie wasn't prepared to tell me anything I didn't need to know.'

Sandon gave a harrumph. 'Fairies,' he muttered. 'Taking my staff.'

The wizard wandered around to the other side of the door, disappearing from view. 'By the Ancient Lords Elemental,' he let out.

'It's not there?' Grim asked him.

'Quite so.'

Sandon reappeared on the other side of the door. 'Now then,' he said to Og-Grim-Dog. 'How many people in Varena did you kill, exactly?'

'Rather a lot,' said Dog sheepishly.

✶

From behind a tree, in the deep dark of night, Og-Grim-Dog watched themselves enter a pig pen. Dog—the Dog from last year, that is—proceeded to smash the pigs over the head with his mace.

Next to them, Sandon strained with the effort required to maintain the illusion, his face red, mouth in a grimace of pain.

Some way farther back in the trees, Raya waited with the families of the small hamlet, anxious faces peering out.

'Looks like we're done,' said Dog, his eyes the sharpest of the three brothers. 'We're talking to one another now.'

'By the Holy Code of Bujutsu,' Sandon got out through gritted teeth, 'can I stop now?'

'Ah. I'm afraid not,' said Grim, having to recall that grisly night all over again. 'We decided to kill the rest of the hamlet, just in case. 'If in doubt, wipe them out.' Those were our orders, you see.'

Sandon gave him a death stare, and for a moment Grim worried that the wizard would turn his magic on them. Instead, with a visible effort, he focused on maintaining and expanding his delicate illusion.

Og-Grim-Dog watched themselves wander over to the sheep paddock.

✻

In Yeggton, they located Karlens Stone, an ex-soldier fallen on hard times. Og-Grim-Dog told him that unless he sobered up, they would eat him; while Raya finished the last of her wine, to make sure it didn't tempt him to fall off the wagon. When she was done she hugged the barrel tight, in a touching farewell.

Yeggton was a thieves' town, full of desperate men. It wasn't so hard finding someone willing to be led to the tattoo parlour with the promise of payment.

'What is it you want?' asked the artist, a short woman who, it seemed, was given to practising on her face while she waited for her next customer.

'He wants every single tattoo he's got,' said Dog, gesturing to Karlens, 'in the exact same place.'

The woman pursed her lips, looking Karlens up and down.

'We can pay,' said Sandon, withdrawing a gold coin.

The new Karlens Stone had a couple of days to heal up before he was sent to The Pressed Apples. Sandon gave him an extra few coin.

'Go and celebrate,' said the wizard.

'Don't mind if I do,' said the man, wasting no time before entering the inn.

'I wonder if I should follow him—' began Raya, before Sandon shook his head at her.

'What have we sent him in there for?' asked the real Karlens anxiously. He was visibly shaking, his face moist with sweat.

38

'Never mind that,' said Dog roughly. 'It's time for you to get out of here. There's a war coming. Learn who the enemy is and gather your troops. Because I've a feeling they'll need you to lead them.'

✳

Og-Grim-Dog led Sandon and Raya across Varena, at each stop undoing the damage they had done the year before. At last, they found themselves once more standing in front of an open door that led to the island of Toyer.

'We did it,' said Grim, satisfied that they had righted some wrongs.

'And what of it?' Og asked. 'When we return to our time, what will have changed? You think that rag-tag band we have saved will be a threat to the Dark Lord by now?'

'Not necessarily,' Sandon answered. 'But ask yourself, if they are so insignificant, why did Lilith have them killed? Why did the Oracle believe they were a threat to the Dark Lord? We have to have faith, that what we have done here will have an influence on the future. Come, time to return.'

They returned to Toyer. There was no fairy waiting for them on their return. Raya did a cursory search of the island but in the end declared that if Elsie wanted to be found, she would be.

The portal on the beach remained. Grim could still see and hear and even smell Varena through it. In the end he decided to close the door.

They made the brief walk to the beach they had arrived on. There was nothing to do now but sit and wait and stare out to sea.

After two days, Raya spotted a cog on the horizon.

AVOLO

The cog was not a big ship, and it took some considerable effort, on everyone's part, to get Og-Grim-Dog back on board without sinking it. It wasn't until the ogre struggled to his feet on deck that the brothers caught sight of the captain.

For a moment, Grim thought he was looking at someone else. It was hard to say what was different about him in a purely physical way. Paler, perhaps; his beard unkempt. It was all about the way he carried himself; the set of his face; most of all, his eyes. They were the eyes of a man who had seen something that had taken away the foundations of their world. As he looked about at the captain's crew, he saw they all had the same kind of look. Lost eyes.

'What's happened?' Sandon asked.

On the journey from Toyer to Avolo, the captain told them what had befallen Gal'azu. In ones and twos, then larger groups, and finally in hordes, the sick of Kuthenia had crossed into the lands of the Free Cities. They were mindless according to the captain, filled with an unnatural, insatiable hunger for flesh—of any kind. It seemed that this hunger had driven them west.

General Caborna, he explained, had been leading sorties out of Avolo to deal with the threat. They had learned, the hard way, that the sickness was transmitted by a bite or scratch. The victim grew ill, and then, over a period of hours or days, transformed into one of the creatures.

'We had more than one outbreak in the city as a result,' the captain said in an emotionless voice. 'Now those who get infected are left. Or put down.'

The captain's story might have been harder to believe, if they had not interviewed the four Kuthenians in Linby.

'They killed that woman, because they knew what she had become,' said Raya.

Sandon nodded. 'And as it turned out, that was just the beginning. The first to arrive from Kuthenia. If the captain talks of hordes in the vicinity of Avolo, then surely there are just as many to the north.'

Grim was surprised to see so many ships active at sea. He supposed that the great merchant fleets that came from far flung destinations overseas weren't to know what was happening in Gal'azu. But he also noticed several vessels, of varying sizes, sailing to or from the Pirate Isles.

When they docked in Avolo, it didn't take long to pick up on the tension in the air. The docks were packed with ships of all sizes and nations. A line of soldiers guarded them, controlling access. Beyond this line, the streets were full, with many citizens and foreigners alike looking over anxiously at the boats.

'Looks like people would like to leave this place,' Og muttered.

Sandon led them off to find General Caborna. They were directed to the city walls.

'Let me show you,' Caborna said, after the briefest of welcomes.

He took them to the eastern section of the walls. Raya was the first to gasp in astonishment at the scene below them. Outside the walls, there truly was a horde. Thousands and thousands of humans, of all ages, pressed against Avolo's defences. If you could still call them humans. Many had been bitten; some half-eaten;

others carried injuries from weapons, or fire, or some other catastrophe. None spoke anything like words: but they groaned, a noise that set Og-Grim-Dog's hackles up. Too stupid, it seemed, to carry weapons, they pushed or punched at the walls with bare fists. Or they clawed at them—breaking nails, blood dripping from fingers. The portcullis, lowered to prevent access to the gate, rattled alarmingly.

'They smell us; or sense us in some other way,' said the general. 'They're harder to kill than you might think. Arrows don't stop them. A piercing blow into the brain, or several blunt strikes to the head are about the only guarantee. Cut off a limb and they carry on regardless. They don't feel pain. Don't seem to need their blood or internal organs to continue.'

'What in Gehenna are they?' Dog asked, appalled.

'They are the undead,' Sandon replied. He stared at the creatures. 'I'm not sure this is a sickness, in the normal sense of the word. Dark magic has been at work here.'

'You think Samael and Lilith did this?' Grim asked him.

'Maybe.'

'But these are Kuthenians,' Og reminded them. 'What would they stand to gain from ravaging an Empire they already control?'

'True enough. I don't know. What news do you have from the rest of the League?' Sandon asked Caborna.

Caborna grimaced. 'Very little. We have been lucky, to some extent, to have the Auster. It has acted as a barrier to them. But these things don't give up and some will have crossed the river.'

'What about Linby?' Grim asked.

The general shook his head. 'I don't know for sure. But I don't see how they can have defended themselves from this. If we didn't have our walls, we'd be finished.' He looked at them, a serious expression on his face. 'I've impounded all naval craft. If we can't hold the city, my plan is to evacuate as many as I can to the Pirate Isles. I already have crews out there, locating and preparing the best sites. I could find a place for all of you. You'd be a very useful addition to our forces.'

Sandon let out a puff of air. 'We are honoured. But—'

'—we have to go back to Mer Khazer,' Raya finished for him.

'We have friends there,' Grim agreed.

GIMME SHELTER

Og-Grim-Dog, Sandon and Raya left Avolo via the West Gate. There was no horde here, but the crowd of undead trying to get in was sizeable enough. It meant that plenty of the creatures must have crossed the Auster and were now at large in the lands of the Free Cities.

When the gates were opened Grim strode forward with purpose—half-measures were likely to get them killed. Dog laid about with his mace, clearing a path through the creatures, Sandon and Raya close behind. Close up, the undead looked terrifying: flesh hanging off bones, their arms reached out to scratch and grab and tear.

Grim kept going, keen to put some distance between them. Once he was sure they were safe, he allowed himself to turn around and look back. Some of the creatures were giving chase: they all had a strange, lumbering gait that meant they moved at a slower pace than Grim could comfortably run. Something in their faces, however—an odd mix of mindlessness and snarling aggression— suggested that they could keep going at that pace without stopping. Others of their kind had given up and returned to pounding on the walls of Avolo.

Grim had seen enough. He wasn't the only one.

'Let's get the shitting crap out of here,' said Raya.

They were sentiments he could completely get behind.

They struck out to the west, in an attempt to outdistance the dead. But it soon became clear that the creatures were already there. They could see them—alone, in twos and threes, in larger groups— on the roads; in the woods; on the plains. Everywhere. Villages and farms lay deserted, their inhabitants either fled or become unfortunate new members of this plague. For it became clear that the creatures they met were as likely to have once been citizens of the Free Cities as Kuthenians. Not that it made any difference where they were from now. Now, they were all one race—a mechanical, witless one, that nevertheless was destroying everything in its path.

They experimented with Raya's Amulet of Hiding, taking turns wearing it. The results were discouraging. Wearing the amulet made no difference. It was as if the undead could locate them using an additional sense to sight or hearing. It was a disturbing idea.

As night drew in, Grim could feel the fear begin to build. There weren't many things that could threaten a group with the abilities they had. But being out here in the dark was surely one. While they were moving, it wasn't too hard to keep a healthy distance from the undead. Once they stopped, however, they would be asking for trouble. It was clear that the dead were drawn to the living like moths to a flame. Except these moths had mouths and were hungry for fresh meat.

'Not sure I can walk through the night,' he admitted, voicing his concerns. Ogres are big units, that need to rest their oversized bodies. For Grim, though—having to carry the extra weight of three heads—it was harder. Og and Dog were able to rest while he was walking, but he had to concentrate. And his legs ached.

'There's a structure over there,' said Raya, pointing into the distance to some location only she could see.

'What do you mean, a structure?' Sandon asked.

'Looks like wooden walls,' said the elf. 'A small fortress, perhaps,' she added, the tone of her voice indicating that she simply wasn't sure.

'Let's try it,' Sandon decided. 'We might get lucky and find a safe place.'

Raya led the way down into a valley. As they neared, they were able to get a good view of the structure she had spotted from afar. Grim found he was looking at a human farmstead. It was surrounded by solid-looking wooden fencing, about the height of an ogre.

'Can't help but think that's been put up recently,' Sandon commented.

Once they got to the floor of the valley, Grim could hear the groans of the undead. Approaching the enclosure, he saw a thin line of them pressing against the panels, which were sturdy enough to withstand the pressure. At the same time, someone stationed on the walls saw them.

'Ogre!' came the rather hysterical scream from a young man who peered over the top of the defence at them. 'There's an ogre come!'

Shouts of alarm from the other side of the fence soon followed.

'Oh dear,' said Sandon. 'Wizards and elves are bad enough. But your presence may just tip these folk over the edge. No doubt they're teetering over the precipice as it is.'

'Maybe you could deal with those undead, Og-Grim-Dog?' Raya suggested. 'It might encourage them to be a little less frightened of you.'

Grim sighed. 'Very well.'

He approached the creatures, who turned around and began to stagger towards him. Even though their experience of fighting the dead was limited, Og-Grim-Dog had already developed a sound strategy. It all revolved around Dog's mace, which could cave in a head in one strike. All Grim had to do was manoeuvre his brother into the best position; while Og used his pike to keep any excess numbers at bay, until it was their turn to meet Dog's mace. The inability of the enemy to block or dodge meant that it was much easier than usual combat, and the brothers were able to make short work of their foe. By the time half a dozen farmer heads were peering at them over the top of the fence, a full dozen undead heads had been crushed to a pulp beneath it.

'Get away, monster!' said one of the farmers, gesturing at Og-Grim-Dog with a wooden spear. Another carried an axe, others, farm tools.

'Steady now,' said Sandon, emerging into view with Raya. The wizard held up his empty hands; though the elf was not about to drop her bow. 'We're just after somewhere to stay the night. We don't want any trouble. You can see the ogre dealt with your undead problem. He's no threat to you.'

'There's no way on this earth that we're letting any of you past these walls,' said the farmer with the axe.

Sandon grimaced, twisting the wrist of one arm. 'We could stay just the one night.'

'You could stay just the one night,' the axeman agreed.

His friend with the spear gave him a punch on the arm. 'He's playing with your mind, you idiot. He's a wizard. Look,' he said, turning to Sandon. 'We appreciate your help and the situation you're in. But we have families in here to protect. There's a barn outside our walls, along that way,' he said, gesturing to a location farther down the fencing. 'It should be safe for one night,' he suggested unconvincingly. 'That's the best offer you'll get from us. Try to break in here and you won't like the outcome.'

Sandon shared a look with Raya. 'Very well. We'll take the barn.'

THE FARM

Once they cleared the barn of undead, it looked like a reasonable place to stay a night. Hay bales offered some comfort, but the wooden planking had seen better days and offered limited security. A watch rota was established to ensure they had good warning of any night-time visitors.

With these precautions agreed, Grim slumped, exhausted, against a stack of hay and fell asleep.

He awoke dazed and confused. For the first moments he didn't even know where he was. Bestial groans and shouts of fear rang out in the darkness.

'Get us up,' he mumbled to his brothers, needing one of them to help him to his feet.

Then there came a sudden burst of pale blue light. It illuminated the barn, reminding Grim exactly where they were and why. Og and Dog helped him to stand, his legs protesting at the sudden requirement to move. He could see Raya nearby, crouching with her hands holding up her bow stave in a defensive stance. She was surrounded by the monsters. Farther away was Sandon, spread-eagled on the floor. He was holding off one of the creatures with one arm, the other stretched up high to cast his spell. More undead shuffled towards him.

'We need our weapons!' Dog said sharply.

Grim felt the vibration as his brother lashed out. Turning, he saw a creature flying through the air. It crashed to the floor of the barn—but it still moved, snarling at them. More of the undead came for them. The barn was full of them.

Grim bent down. 'Grab your mace, Dog!' he shouted. 'Og, keep your hand free. We need to help Sandon!'

As soon as Dog had a firm grip on his weapon, Grim was moving. Og-Grim-Dog was soon onto the undead surrounding Raya, Dog cracking his mace down onto one head after another. With no time wasted, Grim moved on to help Sandon. He sent a vicious kick at the creature the wizard was holding off, powerful enough to send it sprawling away. He bent down and Og picked Sandon up, throwing him unceremoniously over his shoulder.

'There!' Raya shouted, directing Grim to the barn door. It was still firmly bolted. The undead must have got in some other way.

Grim ran for the door. Og—Sandon still balanced precariously on his shoulder—managed to fling away the bolt and Grim crashed through. With Raya by his side, he ran away, pushing himself until his lungs burned and he could run no more. As he gasped for air, Og helped Sandon to slide off and land on his feet.

'Is everyone alright?' Raya asked as she looked about for the enemy.

'No,' said Sandon, his voice shaky and his face pale. Lifting up his robes, the wizard revealed a bite mark on his shin. One of the foul creatures must have got to him as he lay prone on the floor.

Raya gave Sandon a look. 'That's how the infection spreads,' she said.

'I know,' said Sandon. He attempted a rueful smile. 'You may have to leave me here.'

Raya shook her head. 'Og-Grim-Dog, we need to take him to the farm. Get this looked at properly. And we can't take no for an answer this time.'

'Understood,' said Grim.

'I don't think there's anything to be done—' Sandon began.

'—It's my fault,' said Og, interrupting him.

Everyone turned to look at him.

'It was my watch. I fell asleep. I'm sorry.'

'Well,' said Sandon awkwardly. 'If that's the case, I forgive you, Og. It wasn't deliberate.'

Og nodded. 'Thank you, Sandon. Please come to the farm with us. If there's a chance—'

'Alright, Og,' Sandon agreed.

They came to the wooden fencing of the farmstead. Dog cracked his mace against one of the panels, loudly demanding entry. Grim heard the groans and shuffling of the dead in the area, attracted by the commotion.

A head poked over the fence. The spearman from earlier. 'Go away, ogre!' came the shout.

'Our friend is bitten!' Grim fired back. 'One way or another, we're coming in. I suggest you let us in before we smash a hole in your wall and an army of undead follow us through.'

'Wait there,' was the terse response.

They waited, unsure what the farmers were going to do. Dog smashed against the wall, as if they needed reminding a three-headed ogre was outside their home.

Sandon cast another light spell, revealing the approach of the dead.

'Come on!' Dog growled. 'We're not waiting any longer!'

One of the panels was pulled open. Raya grabbed Sandon by the arm and led him through.

'Further!' Dog demanded.

The farmers did as they were told and Grim walked through. He took in the fortified settlement: everywhere along the walls, angled wooden supports held the panels in place. A walkway ran along it too, high enough for the defenders to look out from the walls. All in all, it was an impressive piece of construction.

Inside, towards the centre of the plot, was a typical collection of buildings you would find in a large human farm. Surrounding it were fields for crops and animals. Enough to keep this community going for the time being. Raya and Sandon were already making their way towards the farm buildings, a couple of farmers accompanying them. Those farmers who remained were pushing the fence panel they had opened back into place and then securing it, whilst outside a crowd of undead could be heard, their fingers scratching along the wood.

When the men were done, they turned and stared at Og-Grim-Dog, hands nervously rubbing their sides or fingering weapons, as if they expected the ogre to start biting off heads at any moment.

'We'd like to be with our friend,' said Og, gesturing towards the farm. 'If that's alright with you.'

Most continued to stare as if Og were speaking some other language. But the farmer with the spear gave a reluctant nod. 'Come,' he said. 'There's a chance we can help him.'

No doubt the children of the settlement had been told to stay away from the ogre, but of course they came to peek at Og-Grim-Dog, nonetheless. Sandon had been taken to one of the houses where a woman of the settlement studied the injury by lantern light. Other women and menfolk crowded about and craned their necks around both sides of the ogre to look at the wound and offer their own comments.

'I believe the infection gets into the blood,' the woman said, satisfied that Sandon's only injury was on his lower leg. She was an older woman, hair turned grey, with a reassuring manner about her. 'If it's caught early enough it can be stopped.'

She gestured at one of the women who stepped forward into the light. Her lower arm had been taken at the elbow.

'Marta was bit and survived. We could take yours off at the knee or keep more of the leg by sawing through the bone. Leg bones are not easy to cut through though.'

'By the sprites of Terendael Forest,' Sandon uttered, 'just do what you must.'

'I can cut through his bone, no bother,' Dog offered. 'I've done it plenty of times before.'

The farming folk gasped at this, except the woman, who looked Og-Grim-Dog up and down with no fear. 'Very well. Time is crucial. We can't allow the infection to spread to the rest of the body. Everyone else out!' she commanded, and the house emptied, save for Sandon, the healer and the ogre.

The woman began making some concoction for Sandon to drink, dexterous fingers emptying pouches of herbs and spices into a wooden cup. 'My name is Valeria,' she said as she worked, stirring the ingredients about before handing it to the wizard.

Sandon took it and sipped, making a face. He proceeded to gulp it down.

'We are Og-Grim-Dog,' said Dog. 'And this is Sandon.'

'I am sorry about what happened. These are dark times for Gal'azu.'

The wizard handed her his empty cup. He had a sheen of sweat on his forehead. 'I wonder what it feels like,' he said woozily, 'to turn into one of them.'

'That won't happen,' replied Valeria with confidence. 'Here,' she said, holding his head, 'get some rest.'

Sandon allowed the healer to place his head onto the bed. Within moments he was asleep.

'We must be quick, now, Og-Grim-Dog,' she said. 'Please help me to remove his robes.'

They stripped the wizard. Valeria dipped one finger into a small pot. It came back with a dark, sticky substance which she used to draw a cross on Sandon's leg. She then got on her hands and knees to search under the bed. She retrieved a wicked-looking saw, its teeth long and sharp. She handed the tool to Dog, before continuing her rummaging.

'You want me to start now?' he asked.

Valeria stood with a sigh. 'Yes. Make the cut as smooth as possible. Stop once you're through the bone.' She grabbed a piece of cloth and handed it to Og. 'Mop up as best you can as he cuts. Someone has borrowed my sewing kit. I'll be back shortly to do the mending.' With that, the healer left them to it.

Grim was not generally squeamish, but he found he couldn't watch his friend's leg being hacked into. Instead, he fixed his gaze on Sandon's face; though the sound of Dog's bloody work still came to him, while the back and forth of his brother's arm vibrated through his body. A final scraping noise, and Dog stopped.

'It's done,' he said.

Valeria re-entered the room and looked at Dog's work.

'What have you done?' she asked.

There was something in her voice, a note of alarm and dismay, that worried Grim.

'Cut through already,' said Dog, sounding pleased with himself.

'Cut through the wrong leg!' said Valeria.

'Eh?' said Dog, confused.

Grim made himself look. Shiny white bone and yellow marrow drew his eyes. He looked across at the other leg, where he could plainly see the black cross Valeria had made.

'I marked where to cut!' said the healer, struggling not to lose her temper completely.

'Oh,' said Dog, realisation dawning. 'I thought that was a cross. You know. I thought you meant 'not this one'.'

'Oh Lord Vyana,' Og murmured, a wet rag still in hand. 'What have we done?'

Valeria struggled to take in a deep breath. 'There's nothing else for it,' she said at last. 'That one still has to come off.'

A GOOD OLD APOCALYPSE

They stayed at the farm for a few days after the attack on Sandon, waiting for him to recover from his double amputation. Grim couldn't help but feel that he and his brothers—mainly his brothers, if truth be told—were responsible for the situation that the wizard found himself in. But Sandon was very magnanimous in refusing to apportion blame or dwell on the mistakes that had been made. His focus was on getting well and as each day passed, he became more confident that the radical treatment had worked. The infection had been removed in time and he wasn't turning into one of those grisly creatures. On the fifth day, he and Valeria agreed that he was well enough to be moved, even if he wouldn't be fully healed for months.

The folk of the farmstead had warmed a little to Og-Grim-Dog in the intervening time. It wasn't only that they didn't try to eat anybody—an ogre's strength proved very useful in accomplishing the larger scale jobs that needed doing on the farm. As a result, there didn't seem to be too much resentment at the slightly bigger portion sizes they requested at mealtimes.

Farmers, Grim noted to himself, are resourceful types, and when it was time to go, they presented Sandon with a contraption they had built for him. It was a carrying sack that strapped the wizard to Og-Grim-Dog's back. Ropes tightened about the chest and waist spread the weight remarkably well and Grim was surprised at how light it felt when Sandon tested it.

They said their farewells and the farmers opened one of the fence panels to let them out. Raya went first, using a sword to eliminate the undead that had gathered outside the settlement. The elf had spent her time practising killing the creatures with a bow and arrow—settling on aiming for the eye socket as the most effective way to get the job done. Still, a sharp sword remained a trustier method at close quarters, and everyone was wary of putting Sandon in harm's way again. So Og-Grim-Dog waited until Raya had done her work and then they were away.

As the farmers restored their wall, Og gave them a wave goodbye, which they returned. 'Let's hope those walls hold forever,' he said.

'They're strong walls,' Sandon acknowledged from his perch behind them. 'Capable of holding off hundreds at a time. But thousands?'

Grim didn't say anything. But he had been thinking the exact same thing.

✢

Raya led them northwest towards Mer Khazer. Sandon's bite was a lesson they had all learned now. They avoided the dead whenever possible and stopped travelling when there was still plenty of light, making sure they had somewhere safe to stay the night. As it was, hours of walking were tiring for Grim and painful for Sandon— they were always ready for a rest. Raya hunted and scavenged for food without complaint and she provided enough to keep spirits up.

If they had been catching up to the vanguard of the undead invasion before their stay on the farm, they were far behind it now. The roads were full of the creatures. They staggered ever westwards, some instinct within them sending them after the humans who had abandoned their farms and villages.

That they had left in a hurry was obvious by the things that had been left behind. Some were still in their proper place—others scattered and broken by the monsters who had driven their owners away. In some homes they entered it was possible to imagine that the owners had left on a brief trip and would soon return. Then there were those where crockery and storage vessels lay smashed to pieces, as if the undead had ruined precious possessions out of wilful cruelty. It was sad, to Grim, to see these leftovers of people's lives, even if they were people he had never met. At times he wondered what could be done: if this land might ever be saved, or if the living had permanently lost it to the dead. Most of the time, however, his worries were on a much smaller scale. He thought of Assata, Borte and Hassletoff in Mer Khazer. He hoped that when they reached the town, they wouldn't be too late.

'There's one good thing about it,' said Dog as they rested by the side of a road—Sandon, unstrapped, lay on the ground, rubbing some feeling back into his legs. Raya, meanwhile, had gone off exploring, after spotting something of interest. 'We don't have to wear those head sacks anymore.'

'Yes,' Og acknowledged. 'Though that is because human civilisation has collapsed.'

'And what's that to us?' asked Dog. 'All humans have ever done is try to kill us. Maybe we're looking at this wrong. Maybe a good old apocalypse is an opportunity for the likes of us.'

'I don't recall ever trying to kill you,' said Sandon.

'And what about Assata, and Borte?' Og added.

'I'm not saying that, am I?' Dog said, his temper fraying. 'I'm not arguing against going to Mer Khazer and finding our friends. But what then? If this realm really has collapsed, never to return, we need a plan.' He gazed off into the distance. 'Darkspike Dungeon ain't far from here.'

'Oh no,' said Grim. 'You're not thinking of sitting about in that cavern again?'

'Not sitting about doing nothing. No. But a secure dungeon might not be such a bad place to see this thing out, you know.'

Grim nodded. Maybe it wasn't such a bad idea. And they would have to come up with a plan soon. Wandering about this dead-infested realm every day, searching for a new place to stay every night, was simply too dangerous.

He spotted Raya returning to their position. As ever, she was fleet of foot, making the process of moving at pace look as easy as Grim found it difficult. As she neared, Grim could see she had a serious expression on her face.

'I *thought* I'd seen something,' said the elf. 'Turned out it was Erendael, leading a small group south-east. Taking them to Avolo.'

'Erendael?' Sandon asked. 'Who was with him?'

Raya reeled off another five names, all members of the Bureau.

'Who in Gehenna is Erendael?' Og demanded.

'You know Erendael, Og,' Grim chided. 'He's the only other elf left at the Bureau, other than Raya.'

'Don't recall meeting any other elves,' said Og stubbornly.

'Avolo?' Sandon prompted.

'Yes. I told him we'd come from there—what it was like.' Raya shrugged. 'Didn't seem to put him off. I told him to ask for Caborna. I hope they get themselves on a boat.'

'And Mer Khazer?' Grim asked, anxious for news.

Raya's expression became grim. 'Erendael said Dorwich fell to the undead two weeks ago. A horde crossed the Auster there and they've been to every town and city in the region since. Mer Khazer is no exception. When Erendael left, the undead were already inside the walls. Hassletoff refused to leave, leading the resistance. Fighting them street by street, apparently. But Erendael felt the writing was on the wall. Assata and Borte were both safe and well when he left. But that was two days ago.'

Everyone was silent for a while as the news sank in. It was bad, Grim had to acknowledge. But his worst fears—the kind that come at night when you try to find sleep—well, those hadn't been realized. Their friends were alive two days ago.

Wordlessly, he bent at the knees. His brothers picked Sandon up and the wizard clambered into position. Raya helped to tighten the ropes that held him in place. Then they left for Mer Khazer. For their friends.

HABEAS CORPUS

They weren't the only ones who approached the ruptured walls of Mer Khazer. Lines of the undead were still being drawn there, despite the fact that the town had been invaded days ago. If Grim's conclusions were correct, and the creatures had some supernatural sense that attracted them to the living, their appearance was a mixed blessing. For while it made their quest more dangerous, it suggested that some in the town still lived.

A problem presented itself. As they neared the town, the dead swung around in their direction. Even those creatures that had entered Mer Khazer sensed them and left again—their hunger for living flesh driving them on.

'Come on, Grim,' Raya encouraged. 'If we dally, we'll be surrounded.'

The elf led the way. She had to stop regularly—aiming for the eye socket was the kind of shot where you needed to be still, even for an expert markswoman like Raya. This helped Grim to keep up with her, while Og's pike proved to be useful at keeping the creatures at a safe distance, jabbing out at any that got too close.

Raya cursed as they approached an entrance into the city. The wooden gates had been torn away from the wall here and lay on the ground. A line of the dead stood there, barring the way.

Grim accelerated towards them while Og adjusted his grip to the middle of the shaft, his weapon now held horizontally before him. As Grim charged the line, Og punched his pike forwards, sending the creatures sprawling onto the ground. Grim kept going, offering a silent prayer to Lord Vyana that his ankles or legs weren't bitten. His front foot landed on one of them, and he felt it cracking rib bones and sinking into rotting flesh. He stumbled. Somehow, he righted himself and got to safety.

He turned, allowing Og to pierce the skulls of the undead who returned to their feet with the sharp point of his pike. Raya joined them, agilely passing through the obstacle of flailing limbs.

'Over there!' she cried, pointing down the street that led towards the centre of Mer Khazer.

Once Og had completed his work, Grim looked down the street. At the far end, he could see a large crowd of undead, all facing the other way, into the centre of town. This crowd extended beyond his vision, making it impossible to see how many more there might be. Grim could see the undead at the back trying to shuffle forwards, but it seemed that they were so tightly packed that none of them could get any farther.

'We have to assume that's where the survivors are,' said Sandon. It was an odd sensation for Grim, hearing the wizard's voice come from behind him.

'But we have to be careful,' Raya warned, glancing about. 'It would be very easy for us to get trapped here.'

'Agreed,' said the wizard. 'But what choice do we have?'

Sandon was right. After all their efforts to get here, they were hardly about to turn around and leave.

'Follow me,' said Raya. She led them through the side-streets of the town, approaching the crowd of the dead from another angle. They peered out at one of the main streets of Mer Khazer from a narrow walkway between two shops. Here, they could see that the numbers were much larger than they had seen upon entering the town.

'Thousands of them,' Og whispered.

'They are congregating around the Bureau of Dungeoneering,' Sandon noted.

Indeed, the creatures were scraping their bloody fingers at the frontage of the Bureau and also the two more sizeable buildings on either side: Discount Dungeon Supplies and the gothic grandeur of Nick Romancer's Funeral Parlour. All three showed signs of having been fortified against such an attack—their entrances boarded up with strong planks of wood. The wood creaked as the press of bodies threatened to break through.

'That must be where Assata and the others are,' said Grim. 'But how can we get them out?'

'There is a spell of disguise I could use,' Sandon said, his voice absent of the usual confidence he had when discussing his magic repertoire. 'The Sorcerous Assassins of Al-Rashid devised it, to allow them to enter any enemy stronghold. Cast on ourselves, it makes creatures think we are one of them. If it works on the dead, we would be able to walk straight past them and they would presumably ignore us, just as they ignore one another. But if it doesn't work, and we are bitten...'

Sandon said no more. In truth, nothing more needed to be said. It seemed a pretty desperate sounding gamble to Grim. But they had no other ideas and they were not about to walk away from their friends.

The sound of splintering wood and a great crash could be heard then. The boards nailed across Discount Dungeon Supplies had given in and the undead that were closest poured into the shop. More shuffled into the space that they had vacated.

'If we're going to do it,' said Dog, 'it looks like we need to act sooner rather than later.'

'Who's that?' Raya asked.

As ever, the elf had spotted something or someone no-one else had. Grim peered over to where she gestured. A creature—that at first glance might have been mistaken for one of the dead—was crossing the road near the far edge of the crowd. Except this creature had its hands in its pockets and—if Grim wasn't mistaken—was whistling.

'I think that's our lawyer,' said Og.

They decided to follow Mr Agassi. They caught up with him on the way towards the Old Town, where Grim recalled the lawyer had his house.

'Oh. Hullo,' he responded when they hailed him. He looked more than a little surprised to see them. 'I thought I was the only one left.'

'We've only just arrived,' Grim explained. 'But we think our friends are still here.'

'I see.'

'It would seem the undead are attracted to the living,' said Sandon. 'That's why they are congregating around the Bureau building.'

'Hmm. Sandon, is that you?' asked Mr Agassi.

Grim turned to the side to allow the ghoul a proper view of the wizard.

'Yes. Lost my legs,' said Sandon. 'Long story,' he added, mercifully sparing everyone an account of Og and Dog's ineptitude.

'I'm sorry,' said the ghoul. 'It seems the world has turned. Though I have to say, this New World doesn't treat one such as myself so badly.'

'The undead don't target you?' Grim asked.

'No. And, without wanting to sound too repulsive about it, there's hundreds of meals walking past me every day. All in all, I could have it a lot worse.'

'But don't you miss the law?' Og asked him.

'You know, I didn't think I would. But now I think I kinda do.' Mr Agassi shrugged. 'But what can be done? It seems that the Dead have won this war. Quite easily.'

'Do you think you'd be able to help us?' Grim asked. 'With our friends?'

Mr Agassi frowned, his eyes shining with their green-tinged light. 'If, as you say, the undead are attracted by the living, wouldn't rescuing your friends make my walking meals leave town? Just to play devil's advocate, you understand.'

'It looks very much,' said Raya, 'as if your walking meals will get to our friends soon. And then they'll leave anyway.'

Mr Agassi nodded. 'Point well made. Very well, as a professional courtesy to my clients, I will help. What do you want me to do?'

✻

'Hullo?' Agassi shouted up at the Bureau of Dungeoneering again.

From his hiding place back in the walkway, Grim found it astonishing that despite the huge racket the lawyer was making, the undead—a horde of them, barely five feet away—completely ignored him. Not a flinch. Not even a look his way.

'Is anyone there?' the ghoul continued.

Movement. On the roof—not of the Bureau, but the funeral parlour next door. A small figure appeared and waved down.

'Director Hassletoff!' Mr Agassi called up. 'I have some friends of yours down here, who have been desperate to find you!'

'Who would be mad enough to *enter* Mer Khazer right now?' Hassletoff called down.

The undead moaned at this sudden noise, redoubling their efforts to get into the building on which the halfling perched.

'I have an ogre, an elf and a wizard. Or, at least, most of a wizard,' Agassi added, gesturing to the walkway. 'They are under the impression that you and their other friends need rescuing?'

Hassletoff looked down at the walkway, then gave a little wave. 'Assata and Borte are with me. And one other—the owner of these premises. All unharmed. But we've left it a little late for rescues,' he said, gesturing at the swarm below him. The Director of the Bureau was making light of the situation he was in, but Grim could hear the regret in his voice. 'I am all ears to any ideas about getting them out of here. So long as they don't involve risking someone else's life. Because it was our decision to stay here, not yours.'

'Well, I didn't mean to suggest we had a plan,' Agassi shouted back.

'I see,' said the halfling in a resigned way. He seemed to consider the problem. 'Do you think you would be able to get into Discount Dungeon Supplies?' he asked.

'It's rather busy in there,' said the ghoul. 'But I could try.'

'Before the dead came, the shop was stocked with certain supplies. Including grappling hooks. I can't be sure if there are any left. But if you could get your hands on one and throw the hook up here; perhaps fasten the end to something strong enough near that walkway? It might give us a chance to escape. Though I suspect that as soon as we begin to move, the undead will be on to us.'

Mr Agassi turned to look at them and raised a hairless eyebrow. Like everyone else, Grim gave him a wordless nod. It was the only option on the table.

Agassi approached the crowd of undead who stood outside the entrance to Discount Dungeon Supplies. He began to push and squeeze his way through. Of course, the lawyer believed that the dead would not attack him. But still, Grim thought he was watching something very brave.

At the same time, Hassletoff disappeared back into the funeral parlour. They waited, the undead moaned, and Grim's nerves began to fray. Ogres were made for fighting, not hiding in alleyways.

They emerged at the same time. Hassletoff was the first to appear on the roof of the building. Grim felt a rush of relief to see Assata, then Borte. Lastly, a fourth figure. Nick Romancer was tall and lanky, with a mop of black hair. Meanwhile, Mr Agassi jostled his way out of the packed crowd of undead. He was clutching a grappling hook, a trio of metal spikes attached to a long length of hempen rope. So far, so good.

It took the ghoul a number of tries to get the hook up to the roof of the building—grapple-throwing clearly not part of his legal studies. But his final effort saw the hook land on the tiles and Hassletoff, his light frame sure-footed on a surface that Og-Grim-Dog would simply have fallen through, grabbed it before it rolled away. As their friends set about securing the hook, Agassi took the other end to where Grim and the others were waiting.

'Not sure what we can tie this to,' the lawyer muttered.

'Here,' said Dog, holding out a hand. 'We can't afford to waste time.'

Dog and Og gripped onto the rope. Grim backed away a little until it was taut, his brothers giving their end a good pull to make sure that it was secure at the other end. It held firm.

'Alright,' said Og. 'Could you tell them to get going?' he asked
Mr Agassi.

The ghoul gave the shout and Borte came first, gripping a piece
of cloth that had been tied onto the rope. She slid down towards
them gracefully and at some speed. But as soon as the Kuthenian
princess began to pass over the heads of the undead, they gazed at
her with their vacant faces, emitting their dreadful moans. As one,
they turned and began to follow her towards the walkway.

Relying on Dog to keep his hold on the rope, Og let go and
held out a hand to catch Borte with. He was strong and dexterous
enough to clutch her before she crashed into them, a collision that
would have done her far more damage than them.

Meanwhile, as the undead shuffled towards them, Raya began
to loose her arrows at the closest, aiming for their eye sockets. Her
success rate was high, those hit true falling inert to the ground and
presenting something of an obstacle to those that followed them.
A few inches out, though, and the arrow appeared to do no damage,
sticking out of foreheads, even lodging in the undead's gaping
mouths, the creatures either oblivious or uncaring of the injury.

'Next!' cried Agassi as he moved to meet the oncoming horde.
He grabbed the nearest, throwing it to the floor. Still the creatures
ignored him, as if he wasn't there.

With Borte successfully stashed, Hassletoff was the next to
come sliding down the rope, just as swiftly as she had done.
Although the undead reached for him, he tucked his knees to his
chest and avoided their grasping hands. They appeared to moan all
the more at having missed him and carried on towards Og-Grim-
Dog's position.

'I'm nearly out,' Raya warned as she continued to release the last
of her missiles. In truth, her barrage had slowed rather than stopped
the inevitable advance.

Nick Romancer came next. Grim could tell that his brothers strained more with his weight than the previous two. As he sloped down towards the undead, he tried to avoid their clutches, but his long limbs were inimical to his success and he was grabbed. For a moment in time Grim could see the man stretched out, his hands on the rope and dead hands on his legs. Then his grip failed, and he was pulled down amongst them.

'No!' came a shout from the rooftop, as Assata looped a piece of cloth over the rope and launched herself down it.

'Dammit!' came a voice from behind Grim. He felt Sandon, still strapped to their back, shift his weight. One hand stretched out towards the horde of undead. Then he uttered a second word. 'Blast!'

Suddenly, a huge gust of wind materialised. Sandon had directed it against the undead, but the force of it rocked Grim backwards. He struggled to stay on his feet, relying on his brothers' grip on the rope to keep his balance. Ahead of him, the undead were knocked over by the force of the magic blast, some of them lifted into the air and carried away, bodies crashing into the buildings on the opposite side of the street. Grim looked for Mr Agassi, but he too seemed to have been blown away by the wind. He spied Nick Romancer sprawled out on the street, not blown quite as far as the dead, whose desiccated bodies were perhaps lighter than those of the living.

Just before she reached the funeral director's position, Assata released her hold on her cloth handle and dropped to the ground, landing on her feet in an agile crouch. Wasting no time, she pulled him to his feet. It seemed that he lived, though Grim was well aware that if he had been bitten, he would not remain in that state for long. The barbarian helped him to hobble his way towards them, as behind them the horde of the undead regained their feet. Not killed by Sandon's spell, then. But hopefully scattered enough for them to make their getaway.

'What's happened to Sandon?' Borte asked with alarm.

'Oh, he's just had his legs chopped off,' Dog said in a reassuring voice.

'Og-Grim-Dog, he's not conscious,' said Raya, her voice just as worried as Borte's.

'We need to go,' said Hassletoff, his voice harsh and commanding. 'We can't waste time here.'

As Assata and Nick staggered over, Og and Dog gripped the man and unceremoniously swung him over Dog's shoulder.

'What about Mr Agassi?' Grim asked.

Everyone looked, but no-one spotted him, not even Raya.

'We must leave him,' said the elf. 'Assume that he is safe and unharmed. It makes no sense risking a bite for someone who doesn't get bitten.'

'Come,' said the Director of the Bureau, not waiting to see if they followed, but striding down the walkway.

Grim followed, weighed down by a wizard and the owner of a funeral parlour. With him came an elf, a barbarian and a princess.

Once again, Og-Grim-Dog found themselves leaving Mer Khazer. This time, however, it really felt like they were leaving for good.

MESSAGES

They made their way south of Mer Khazer, no real thought as to their destination. They were simply trying to put some distance between themselves and the horde of undead that followed. For behind them, the creatures spilled out of Mer Khazer. With no living left in that town, they would now wander Gal'azu, searching for their next victims.

The group travelled mostly in silence, until they had got far enough away that it felt safe to stop for a rest. They found a spot where a meadow met a copse of trees, a place that felt like it offered a degree of comfort and safety. Assata helped Og-Grim-Dog to lower Nick Romancer and Sandon to the ground, before Grim sat down himself, exhausted.

Raya put a hand to the wizard's forehead while searching for a pulse. 'He lives,' she said. 'But that spell cost him. He wasn't yet recovered from his injuries.'

'What happened to him?' Borte asked, staring at Sandon's shortened legs.

Raya and Grim shared a brief look. 'That's a story for later,' said the elf. 'What about him?' she asked, gesturing at Nick Romancer, sat with his back against a tree.

'He's very white,' Dog whispered to his brothers.

'He's wearing make-up,' said Og.

Grim studied the human. Now that his brother had mentioned it, he *could* see the white foundation, with bright colour about the eyes and cheeks.

'Why in Gehenna is he wearing make-up?' Dog demanded.

'Because he wants to,' said Og sharply.

Assata was checking Nick over, his tunic lifted as she inspected his bare torso.

'I'm sorry,' the barbarian murmured, sounding absolutely distraught. 'They bit you. More than once.'

It appears Assata really likes this man, Grim noted to himself. *Though I can't recall her mentioning his name even once before we left to visit the Oracle.*

The undertaker closed his eyes, nodded to himself, then opened them again. 'I thought so,' he said, resigned.

'We can chop them off,' Dog offered. 'That's what happened to Sandon, and it worked. The sickness didn't spread.'

'We can't chop off his back; his shoulder; his neck,' said Assata sorrowfully.

'Ah.'

'It's a shame we don't have Brother Kane or some other healer with us anymore,' said Hassletoff sombrely. 'We need such skills more than ever.'

'Where *are* all the other citizens of Mer Khazer?' Raya asked him. 'The adventurers; townsfolk; the Kuthenians? We met Erendael on the way here but have not seen or heard from anyone else.'

'Erendael and his companions were some of the last to leave. When I heard that Dorwich had fallen, I told people to start leaving Mer Khazer. Most went west, in the end. To Magidu. It seemed like the safest option.'

'Then why did you four stay so long?' Og asked the halfling.

Hassletoff glanced towards the undertaker. 'We hoped that Nick might find a cure.'

'A cure?' Raya asked.

'I was working on an elixir that might end this sickness. Even a medicine to protect the living would have been something. As I laboured at my research, Assata, Borte and Hassletoff stayed with me. Protected me when the town was overrun. But I failed.'

'And what do you know of black magic?' asked Grim suspiciously.

Nick grimaced. 'It is true. I have been driven to study the Dark Arts, for my sins. I learned of the draugr, sometimes called *again-walkers*. Men whose will returns to its body after death. But the sorcery I learned wasn't enough to stop this plague.'

'It's not your fault,' said Assata. The barbarian looked around. There was no doubting she had changed. When they had left Mer Khazer for the Oracle, Assata was full of righteous rage. Now she seemed broken. 'Is there a plan now?' she asked. 'A destination anyone has in mind? What came of your quest to see the Oracle?' she asked, a trace of the old bitterness still there.

'Erendael was heading for Avolo,' said Raya. 'We came from there. The city was still intact when we left, but severely threatened. Caborna was developing an escape plan—to sail as many as he could to the Pirate Isles.'

Assata sneered at the mention of the general's name.

'Who knows whether the city stands or whether Caborna has abandoned it by now?' Raya added.

'How did a meeting with the Oracle take you to Avolo?' Hassletoff asked.

'I think that's a story to share over the fire tonight,' said Raya. 'I suggest we do our best to make a comfortable camp here. Gather what supplies we can before night falls. And take care—the dead

are drawn to the living. We need at least one person to take guard
duty from now on.'

✻

Og-Grim-Dog woke their camp. It was wet and grey—but
morning, nonetheless. Time to move.

They had taken the last watch of the night. After what had
happened to Sandon, Raya had suggested that they take watch
together. And it was hard to argue. Only one of the undead, that
Nick Romancer had named *draugr*, had come. A female human,
skin puffy and swollen, her lower jaw missing, so that Grim
wondered whether she was still capable of biting anyone. Still, Dog
had finished her off, just in case. For whatever reason, such
encounters held more terror in the night. They had escaped a horde
of the creatures in Mer Khazer, yet Grim found himself still
thinking of that individual draugr for days afterwards.

Last night, Og-Grim-Dog and Raya had told the others of their
adventures. Firstly, the words of the Oracle of Britrona. *The dead
are restless. Hungry. The living are scattered. Lost. It is the end
times.* How she had sent them south, to an uninhabited island off
Xaritja. How they had met Elsie, Guardian of the Portals, who had
allowed them to travel backwards in time to Varena, where they
had righted the wrongs committed by Og-Grim-Dog last year.

'Where does that leave us?' Hassletoff had asked when they were
done. 'You saved those people who Lilith wanted killed. But what
of these draugr? What can we do about them?'

'I don't know,' Raya had admitted. 'Maybe when Sandon wakes
up, he will have an idea.'

Well, Sandon was awake now. Groggy and a little disoriented,
but able to take his breakfast when Borte helped him with it.

73

Nick Romancer was also still in the land of the living. For now. Grim had noticed that the undertaker's sleep had been troubled, and he had woken with a sheen of sweat on his forehead, his flop of dark hair wet with moisture. Assata tended to his needs, helping him to his feet. Grim was relieved to see that he could walk unaided.

The early morning ministrations were interrupted by Raya, who had gone scouting as soon as Og-Grim-Dog had woken her.

'Trouble,' she said, her voice tense. 'A crowd of draugr, heading straight for us. I'm pretty sure they've followed us from Mer Khazer. We need to move.'

'All of them followed us?' Hassletoff asked.

'No. Not the entire horde. But hundreds. Too many to fight off, that's for sure.'

No more persuasion was needed. Raya helped to get Sandon into his carrying sack. By the time the wizard was securely attached to Og-Grim-Dog's back, Grim could hear the distant groans of the draugr.

Hassletoff and Borte led the way, with Og-Grim-Dog following; close behind came Nick Romancer, propped up by Assata; while Raya took the rearguard position, keeping an eye on the enemy that followed them.

'We still don't know where we're going,' Assata reminded everybody.

'Avolo is a long way to walk, with uncertain outcome,' came Sandon's voice, dry and weak sounding, but a welcome sound to Grim's ears, nonetheless. 'If we head due south we can get to the coast. There are settlements there, hopefully less touched by this disaster, where there is a good chance to find a boat.'

'What do we need a boat for?' asked Assata. 'Why not escape westwards?'

'We need to find a boat,' Sandon repeated. He said no more—couldn't or wouldn't, Grim didn't know which.

So Hassletoff led them south. They walked, rarely stopping, putting back some distance between themselves and the draugr, but never enough to feel safe. The countryside about Mer Khazer was a mix of wooded hills and valleys, with flat stretches of plains and meadows. Regularly spaced about this gentle countryside were farmsteads, hamlets and sizeable villages. Enough had been left behind for the group to keep their food supplies topped up, but while they occasionally ran across small groups of draugr, they never encountered the living.

Until they did. Sort of.

The first time, they thought nothing of it. One word, *Babylon*, scrawled across the wooden wall of a house, accompanied by a hand painted arrow. It could have meant something, or nothing. But next time, the author had the whitewashed wall of a village church to work with, and the message was a bit more elaborate. *Find Sanctuary in Babylon. We are safe.* And there was another arrow.

'The arrow is pointing in the same direction as the other one,' Raya noted.

'What do you mean?' Assata asked her.

The elf raised an arm in front of her. 'Standing before this message, I am facing due south. The arrow is pointing to the south-east. The arrow on the other house indicated the exact same direction.'

'So, they are suggesting we head in that direction?' Grim asked. He looked to the south-east, finding nothing but more of the Great Outside.

'Why would we do that?' asked Dog. 'It could be a trap.'

'Nick can't go on much longer,' said Assata.

Grim knew very well what Dog thought of that. The man was going to die anyway.

'Sandon needs rest, too,' said Raya.

That was a little different.

'Then we should see if we can find this Babylon?' Hassletoff asked, twirling his moustache. 'Even if all we get is a night's sleep behind strong walls, it would be worth it.'

Everyone looked at one another. Tired faces stared back. Some haunted looking.

'I'll take that as a yes,' said the halfling.

BABYLON

Someone has been busy,' Raya commented as they approached the sanctuary of Babylon.

At first, all Grim saw was a hill. Only when he got closer, did he see the evidence of human construction. Great earthworks followed the contours of the mound in concentric rings. Tall enough, and sturdy enough, to keep out the draugr.

'I'm guessing there's an entrance to the fort somewhere,' said Hassletoff.

The halfling looked up to the top of the hill. A palisade of wooden stakes made it difficult to see what lay up there. Grim supposed that the inhabitants might not take kindly to them climbing up the earthen banks without warning.

'Then let's find it,' Assata said.

So, they circled the walls, looking for a gap in the solid defences.

'If we weren't seen at first,' said Og, with a glance upwards, 'we have been now.'

The first sign they found was a white chalk path, running south-north to the hill. Then, the familiar moans of draugr. Og and Dog readied their weapons, as did the ogre's companions. As they came around a sharp bend in the base of the hill, the entrance was revealed. The chalk path rose upwards and ended in a giant cleft in the earthworks. The defences reared up, three sheer vertical walls, impossible to climb. It was less of an entrance than it was a dead end.

But Grim had little time to think more on that. Congregating at the foot of this great cleft were about a dozen draugr. Somehow drawn to this location, and presumably to the people who lived at the top of the hill fort, it seemed they had simply gathered at the bottom, unable to get closer. Now, though, they sensed newcomers. Og-Grim-Dog and his friends were closer than the people on the hill. They were out in the open, too. The creatures began to lurch their stiff bodies towards them.

Grim led his friends into an attack. They had learned they needed to fight them with care. A bite, maybe even a scratch, and they would get the same infection that Nick Romancer suffered with. Og used his pike to keep the draugr at bay and Borte used her spear. Assata and Hassletoff both used shields with their swords to give themselves an extra source of protection. Raya, meanwhile, used her bow and arrow to fight at long range. She was getting better at targeting the draugr's eye sockets—the only location where her arrows could reliably do enough damage to kill the creatures. For those who fought in the melee, the goal was to hack or stab cold iron into the skulls of the creatures. It seemed to be the only thing that worked, for while chopping off limbs disabled the draugr, it didn't stop them.

Once they had eliminated a good number of the draugr, Grim dared to move in closer. He was less agile than normal with a wizard strapped to his back, and agility had never been his strong point in the first place. Now Dog used his mace to finish them off, a swift crack to the head enough to knock them to the ground and keep them there. Og used his pike to prod at the bloated, half-decomposed corpses, making sure they were not going to rise once more.

'Safe,' he declared.

Assata went to fetch Nick Romancer, who had watched the skirmish from a seated position. She helped him to his feet, unsteady like a new-born colt.

'There's someone up there,' came Sandon's voice from behind Grim.

Everyone walked over to the cleft in the earthworks and bent their necks to peer up to the top of the fort. Grim could see a small figure leaning over the precipice, too high up to tell who or what it was.

'Thanks for eradicating our pest problem!' a human man's voice floated down.

For some reason, the company looked at Og-Grim-Dog to respond for them. Grim supposed that the loudness of an ogre's voice might have something to do with it.

'No thanks necessary, we enjoyed it!' Dog shouted up.

'Are you the one who wrote the signs?' Og asked.

'Yes.' There was a slight pause. 'Are you a two-headed ogre?' came the voice. Grim thought he could detect an air of concern.

'No!' Dog shouted. 'We have three heads!'

'Oh.' For some reason, that didn't seem to reassure the man. 'You're not going to be trouble, are you?'

'Og-Grim-Dog is perfectly safe,' came Sandon's voice, far louder than usual. 'You've invited people here, are you going to deny us entry now?'

'When I did the inviting, I didn't intend to include ogres. I'm not sure how popular that will be with the other citizens of Babylon. Do you have any bitten with you?'

'Yes,' shouted Dog. 'We have one. Well, there's a second, too, but we chopped his legs off.'

'Oh, that's no good. The bitten turn into the undead.'

'We're aware of that,' Sandon replied, an edge to his voice.

'Well I can't let them into Babylon. We have few hard and fast rules, but that's one of them. The safety of those here has to come first.'

'I'll stay with Nick,' said Assata, her voice pitched just loud enough for their company to hear.

'We'll stay with you,' Grim offered. 'It'll let those up there get used to the idea of allowing an ogre up.'

'I'll stay too,' said Borte.

'We can't all stay down here,' said Assata, an impatient edge to her voice.

'Alright,' Borte agreed, a hurt expression on her face.

'I'm sorry,' Assata said immediately. 'I'm just exhausted. But I shouldn't snap at you like that.'

Borte nodded and put her hands to her mouth. 'Some of us will come up,' she shouted.

The figure at the top of the fort threw something down. A rope ladder, that reached all the way down to the ground.

'Here, I'll help with Sandon,' said Raya, unstrapping the wizard's carrying sack. 'Sorry, old friend,' she said to the wizard, 'but none of us are strong enough to take you with us.'

Og and Dog carefully placed Sandon on the ground, a safe distance from the increasingly ill-looking undertaker.

Borte, Hassletoff and Raya proceeded to climb the ladder, each as nimble as the other, and they soon disappeared over the edge of the hilltop. The ladder was then slowly reeled back in, leaving Og-Grim-Dog and the others stranded at the bottom.

*

It wasn't easy to watch Nick Romancer deteriorate. Too ill to move now, he sat propped up against the earthen bank of the hillfort.

Too ill to eat, then too ill to drink. First too tired to talk, then too tired to keep his eyes open. His breathing became a loud panting noise.

Assata, Og-Grim-Dog and Sandon waited with him. There was nothing else to do, except when a draugr or two would appear, shuffling their way towards whatever scent the living gave off. Grim would get to his feet and Dog would swing his mace and then it was back to the waiting.

At first, it was barely noticeable when the undertaker passed from the land of the living to the land of the dead. He was breathing and then he wasn't. Then it became rather more noticeable. Nick's eyes flicked open again. Something about them had changed. Glazed over—had they changed colour, too? He looked about him. His face distorted into a snarl. He could move again now, pushing himself to his feet.

'I will do it,' Dog offered.

'No,' Assata replied. 'I need to.'

Her sword strike was clean and the draugr collapsed back to the ground.

'I'm sorry,' she whispered to the corpse.

'It wasn't your fault,' Og offered.

Assata gave a bitter looking smile. 'Will you help me bury him?' she asked.

✶

It wasn't long after Nick Romancer was in the ground that the rope ladder was dropped from the top of the hill fort a second time. This time, someone climbed down instead of up. It was a human man and Grim supposed it was the same one who had refused to lower it earlier.

He moved with confidence and speed, as if he were used to it. When he reached the ground, Grim got a proper look at him. Nothing special, was his first impression. He didn't have the look of a warrior. He was slim, no more than average height, and while clearly an adult human, still had youthful looking features.

'I am Belus,' he introduced himself, his voice more powerful than Grim had expected. 'Founder of Babylon,' he said grandly, waving a hand at the hill behind him.

Belus took in five rather unimpressed expressions. 'I'm sorry about your friend,' he said. 'But we don't let the infected into our fort. Too many of us have lost people after making a mistake like that.'

'Understandable,' said Sandon. He gestured at the place where his legs should have been. 'We've had the same experiences as you.'

Belus nodded. 'I'm sorry for what you have lost. But I can offer you sanctuary now. The monsters out there can't reach Babylon.'

'You wrote those signs—in the villages and farms we passed through?' Grim asked.

'Yes. When this plague first hit Gal'azu, I had a vision from Marduk. I was quick to understand that the dead who drove us out of our homes would end our way of life. Towns, villages, lonely farms—they weren't safe. But I knew how our ancestors survived in this place when they first arrived here all those years ago. When there were more monsters than humans in these lands. They lived in the great hillforts, designed above all to keep themselves safe. These forts were abandoned when life got easier—their isolation had become more of a drawback than a benefit. But in these times, they will be the path to our salvation.'

'How do you know all this?' asked Og.

'From reading. I was a monk before all this started, you see. I spent every spare moment I had in the scriptorium.' Belus's face darkened. 'All lost now. But I learned about the history of Gal'azu. When the undead came, I knew I had a responsibility to use my knowledge to save humankind.' He gave a little smile. 'And it seems it's not only humans I'm saving now.'

'You're a priest?' asked Dog. 'Then why didn't you come and save our friend?'

Belus gave another smile, though he looked a little nervous at Dog's aggressive tone.

'Not one of those kinds of priests, unfortunately. No special healing powers. Just an ordinary man, who dedicated his life to Marduk. Our monastery was overrun, and my life was taken away from me; just like everyone else here. I'm trying to build a community that can survive this catastrophe. If we're going to make it, we need to get stronger. Hence my messages, inviting people to come and join us. Would you like to come and see?'

Assata gave a grunt, which everyone took to be an affirmative, and they made ready. The barbarian and the monk helped Sandon into his carrying sack and attached it to Og-Grim-Dog, making doubly sure he was secure. It wouldn't do to have him fall out during the climb.

'Do you need help getting up?' Belus asked the ogre.

'We'll be fine,' said Grim. 'We just need to take our time. You go up first and we'll follow.'

The ascent reminded Grim of the time they had to clamber down the netting at Wight's Hollow. It took a great deal of care and attention, and an equal amount of cursing, to co-ordinate Og and Dog's hands—letting go of the rope ladder and reaching up for the next rung—and Grim's feet, using the rungs as footholds. It was just as well that they ironed out the kinks at the beginning, for the higher they climbed, the more likely a mistake would be fatal.

Finally, hands reached out for them, and Og-Grim-Dog was hauled onto the summit of the hill.

'Welcome to Babylon,' said Belus.

Grim got to his feet. He was standing inside the palisade of wooden stakes. Raya, Borte and Toff had come to greet them—indeed, had helped the ogre drag themselves onto the top of the hill. A little farther away, a crowd of humans eyed Og-Grim-Dog's arrival in their home with uncertainty.

'Behave yourselves,' Grim reminded his brothers, talking under his breath. 'No sudden movement or loud noises.'

Babylon was a large space, unusually flat. Perhaps, Grim reasoned to himself, if the place had been occupied in ages past, Belus and his people had found it already flattened for them. It was a mix of green grass, and mud and straw in the more well-trodden places. Small wooden dwellings had been built for the inhabitants—no more than twenty of these. Grim could see some evidence of other works, too. A large fire-pit in the centre, and some pens, which contained a sorry looking collection of livestock. Still, Grim supposed, the residents deserved some credit for getting them up here in the first place.

Most impressive, though—to Grim's mind—was the view. Babylon lorded it over this part of Gal'azu. The inhabitants had clear sight in all directions, giving them a chance to control the territory about their fort. It wasn't an ogre's natural choice of refuge—that would have been somewhere underground. But Grim had to concede that the place had potential.

'It's very good,' he said carefully.

'Here,' said Raya, reaching over. 'Let's unstrap Sandon and let him have a proper look.'

Standing certainly felt easier once Sandon had been removed from Grim's back. A wave of exhaustion hit him. The thought of lying down somewhere safe for the night suddenly felt very appealing.

'So,' said Assata. 'I presume this community you are making will rely on hunting?'

'To a large extent, but not exclusively,' Belus replied. 'You see, the thing about these monsters is—'

'Draugr,' said Og.

'Eh?' asked the monk, not following.

'They're called draugr. Nick told us so.'

'Oh, I see. I did not know that. Alright, the thing about the *draugr*, is, they only hunt for living flesh. They completely ignore crops and other edibles. So, in theory, there is nothing to prevent us from farming down below during the daytime and retreating to Babylon at night-time. Come, let me introduce you to our citizens and I can show you some of our plans.'

Assata followed Belus. She fell in next to Borte and placed a hand on the Kuthenian's shoulder. Borte brushed the barbarian's hand with her own, and then they parted.

Hmm, Grim thought to himself as everyone else began to follow them. *I thought Assata had taken a fancy to Nick Romancer. Seems that her affections lie elsewhere.*

Dog gave a whistle. 'Now we know!' he chortled with childish glee.

Assata and Borte turned around and stared daggers at Dog, who wasn't in the slightest bit intimidated, grinning at them stupidly.

Behind Grim came the sound of someone clearing their throat as loudly and unpleasantly as an orc. He turned to look. 'Oh, we do apologise, Sandon,' he said, and Og-Grim-Dog gathered up the wizard in their huge hands and carried him into Babylon.

A NEW COMMUNITY

Over the next few days, Og-Grim-Dog and his friends took the opportunity to catch their breath after the frantic pace at which they had lived their lives. Gradually, they found themselves integrating into the community of Babylon. Raya began to lead hunting parties out into the countryside around the fort. They would return before dark, almost always bringing something back. Sometimes it was fresh meat; sometimes they had caught animals that could be farmed—limbs tied together, they would be winched up using the rope ladders and added to the growing collection of livestock.

Belus soon found he had colleagues with more experience than himself in managing communities. Hassletoff and Borte took the monk's ideas and began to turn them into reality, marking out fields down below, organising the community in the agricultural tasks of ploughing, planting, irrigating. Og-Grim-Dog and Assata welcomed the physical labour this entailed. They would also bring down trees and get the timber back up to the fort, and had soon built houses for their group to live in.

It was unfortunate that Sandon had little involvement in these tasks. There was, of course, the barrier of his reduced mobility. In addition, however, the wizard was less interested in Babylon than the others. Grim wondered at it. One might think Sandon had most to gain from the safety of a community such as this. But when they spoke with him on an evening, gazing over the landscape laid out around them, safety wasn't something that concerned him.

On this particular evening, Og-Grim-Dog were on guard duty at the front of the fort, the huge drop down to the bottom of the hill mere feet in front of them.

'We mustn't forget the real enemy,' Sandon told them, seated in a wooden chair that Assata had built for him. 'The threat from Lilith and Samael isn't any less just because this plague is upon us.'

'Though surely they must be facing a draugr invasion, same as us,' said Dog. Grim's brother had his mace at the ready. They were waiting for Hassletoff and Belus to return to the hillfort before pulling up the rope ladder for the night. 'Don't seem like the dead distinguish amongst the living.'

'Quite possibly true,' said Sandon. 'But as terrible as the draugr seem right now, you need to understand that a succubus and incubus at large in Gal'azu is much worse. Draugr can be killed— returned to the land of the dead. Quite easily, in fact. I'm not sure that Lilith and Samael can be stopped.'

'But I thought we solved that problem when we saved the life of Karlens Stone and those others we killed whilst working for the Dark Lord,' said Grim. 'What else needs to be done?'

'The more I think on it,' Sandon mused, 'the more I think there is for us to do. Those individuals we saved had the *potential* to overthrow the Dark Lord. But that doesn't mean they will just do so on their own. They need our guidance. We are the only ones who know the true nature of the new Dark Lord. Indeed, if we fail to warn them, we may be setting them up to fail.'

'So we must return to Varena?' Og asked.

'Perhaps so,' said the wizard. He held the ogre's gaze with his sharp eyes. 'If the worst happens, and you feel lost, remember the portals on Toyer island. We used them to change history once. Maybe it can be done again.'

A small head appeared at the edge of the hill, before the rest of Hassletoff appeared. Close behind came Belus.

'Success?' Grim asked them.

'Great plans afoot!' beamed the halfling. 'Barley growing. This time next year, Babylon should be well stocked with beer.'

The former Director of the Bureau of Dungeoneering looked at ease in his new role as head farmer. Grim glanced at Sandon. It would be so easy to fall into this new life. But some warning sense told him that the wizard was right. Their work wasn't done.

✻

Og-Grim-Dog had their own bed, with a straw mattress. They had three pillows, just like that time on the barge from Dorwich to Linby. It was the comfiest room they had enjoyed since leaving Fell Towers. So, it was perhaps no surprise that it took them a while to wake from their sleep. In the end, though, the noise at the hillfort forced Grim to open his eyes and sit up. Bloodcurdling screams tend to have that effect.

Dog grabbed his mace; Og his pike; and Grim barged his way out of their new house to take in the scene at the hillfort. It was still dark and Grim determined it was the middle of the night. It made it hard to work out what was going on. But amid the cries of terror, Grim heard the moans of draugr, and that told Og-Grim-Dog most of what they needed to know. As his eyes adjusted to the light on the hilltop, Grim began to make out the shuffling figures that had invaded the fort.

'Ready?' he asked.

'Ready,' said Og and Dog.

Grim's first target was a single draugr, dragging its dislocated leg between two houses. He approached from behind and Dog was able to take it out with a single blow before the creature even realized they were there.

Next, Grim heard screams coming from one of the houses. He found the doorway crammed with draugr. Og spitted the nearest, his pike smashing clean through dry bones. He pulled his catch closer until Dog could reach its head with his mace. The nearest creatures now turned and came at them. The doorway forced them to approach slowly and it was an easy thing for Dog to finish them off one at a time.

'Careful,' Grim nonetheless warned him. 'I heard people in there.'

When the column of approaching draugr was dealt with, Grim risked entering the dark of the house. Several of the creatures were still in there, along with a similar number of desperate human defenders. Og-Grim-Dog was able to attack while their attention was elsewhere. It didn't take long until the last lay crushed under Dog's mace. Grim took in the traumatised expressions of those inside. He could see more than one red wound. But he had no time to offer comfort, for the fort was still overrun.

Emerging from the house, he found Hassletoff dismantling a draugr. Not able to reach the head of his opponents at first, the halfling was required to hack away their legs until he was able to deliver the killing blow. Still, he appeared to be doing an effective job of it with no complaint.

'Og-Grim-Dog!' Hassletoff called out. 'Come, I'm worried about Sandon!'

Sandon. Groggy from being woken from his sleep, Grim hadn't considered the wizard. His lack of mobility made him more vulnerable. He followed the fast disappearing halfling towards his friend's house. He hadn't gone more than a few steps when a sudden explosion lit up the scene: blues, oranges, violets and reds briefly filled the hilltop, revealing the desperate chaos of the fighting like a moment caught in time. A sound like thunder came with it.

'Sandon's house,' said Grim, noting the source of the explosion. He went faster, the multi-coloured image of the hilltop in his mind's eye reassuring him that there were few draugr nearby.

There was little left of the house. Blackened planks had scattered in all directions, some still smouldering from the blast. Hassletoff was kneeling by Sandon, gently raising him to a seated position.

The wizard looked from the halfling to the ogre as Grim approached and crouched down. 'Too late, I'm afraid,' he said, gesturing at the debris from the explosion. 'They got me.'

He gestured to his chest and shoulders, where Grim could see his tunic had been torn away and his flesh ripped open.

'I'm sorry,' said Grim, the words sounding entirely inadequate to his ears.

His brothers mumbled their own commiserations. There would be no chopping off limbs to save their friend this time.

Sandon nodded, acknowledging their words. 'How did they get up here?' he asked.

It was a good question, one that Grim hadn't had a chance to think about until now.

Hassletoff gave them a look. 'You *did* pull the ladder up, didn't you?'

'The ladder?' Dog repeated, his brow furrowing.

Grim tried to remember. He had been talking with Sandon. Hassletoff and Belus had ascended the ladder, the last ones to return to the fort. That was when they should have pulled the ladder back up. Had they done it?

'I don't recall,' he admitted.

'Me either,' said Og.

Well, that was no surprise.

'It's alright,' said Sandon. 'Toff and I were there too. We could have done it as well.'

Hassletoff nodded an acknowledgement. Though, in truth, Og-Grim-Dog had been the ones on guard duty. It had been their responsibility.

The wizard gave his old friend a look. 'There is nothing to gain in having people point the finger of blame. Understood?'

'Yes, Sandon,' said Hassletoff.

'Now, go and finish the job of clearing this place. I'll still be here when you're done.'

INTERMISSION

The Landlord of the Testicles paused a little at this point in his story. A deathly silence hung in the air. This was not the tale the audience had been expecting. They had expected some laughs and some brave exploits from their hero. Yet here was Og-Grim-Dog, admitting that their friend would die as a result of their own dreadful and really rather ridiculous mistakes.

'The rest of the fort was cleared of draugr,' said the third head, his voice a strained monotone. 'We were relieved to find the rest of our friends had survived unharmed.'

The Testicles relaxed a little at this statement, releasing a collectively held breath. They had been worried about the fate of the other characters in the story. For while it was clear that Og-Grim-Dog himself had survived the terrible times he described—he was standing before them, after all—there were no such guarantees for anyone else.

'The people of Babylon decided to change their normal rules, regarding those who had been bitten,' the middle head continued. 'Otherwise, we would have had to send more than a score of poor unfortunates down to the bottom of the hill and wait for more draugr to come for them. At least that was something. Instead, we waited with Sandon, giving him company in his final moments. In the end, Raya Sunshine insisted that she would be the one who finished him when he turned. We waited for it to happen—' he began, but it seemed his words caught in his throat.

'There was an unspoken hope among us,' took up the first head. 'That because Sandon was a wizard, the illness might not affect him in the same way as it had others. But it did, and the elf performed her terrible task. Sandon left a gap in our lives that could not be filled. He had been the one to give us direction in those stormy seas of the first days and weeks of the plague. Now there was a palpable feeling that we were lost; rudderless.'

The Recorder tapped quill on parchment, evidently agitated by something.

'What is it?' asked the third head in a weary voice.

'Let's say for the sake of argument, you forgot to pull up that rope ladder,' the Recorder began, full of inquisitive energy. 'How, by—'

'—the twenty-three circles of fiery Gehenna?' prompted the first head.

'Very well. How in Gehenna did the draugr climb up the rope ladder and get into Babylon? Every description you have given to this point suggests that they are clumsy, barely conscious, shuffling, hebetudinous creatures.'

'I don't recall using the word hebetudinous,' muttered head three.

'Now, suddenly,' the writer pursued, 'a whole herd of them can climb forty feet up a rope ladder!'

'Well, it's an inconsistency,' said the middle head of the ogre.

'I know that!' spluttered the Recorder. 'But I have come to find out the truth. To sift the facts from the fabrications, to peel back the layers of myth-making, the exaggeration and the misrepresentation; to record for posterity, what really happened. How can I do that if you just shrug and say it's an inconsistency!'

'I think you're being very harsh,' said the third head. 'Read any work of fiction or non-fiction and you're liable to come across one or two examples. We are simply recalling our collective memories of these events. As we have explained, we didn't see the draugr climbing the rope ladder. We awoke to find them already in the fort.'

'Yes, but what am I supposed to write? How to make this event believable to the reader?'

'Frankly,' said the middle head, 'that is your job. It is not our job to suggest what may or may not have happened when our backs were turned, or we slept. Sometimes, in life, the inexplicable simply happens. And you just get on with it. This is one of those occasions. Now, shall we proceed?'

The Recorder's lips disappeared into his mouth for a while as he meditated on the ogre's words, before he relented. 'Please, continue.'

THE NIGHT FIRE

'Here,' said Raya as they gathered after the funeral.

'Sandon's Ring of Curse-Breaking?' said Og. 'Why are you giving it to *us*?'

The elf shrugged. 'He said you should have it. I think he still had the idea that one of us might return to the portals on Toyer and have need of a payment for Elsie.'

'But we're the ones responsible for his death,' said Dog despondently.

'Maybe that's why he wanted you to have it.'

Dog frowned in confusion. But Grim thought he understood. Sandon was a clever and an honourable man.

✳

The community at Babylon was given precious little time to get back on its feet after the attack. A week later, Grim found himself awake in the night again. At first, he assumed that the noises signalled another night-time visit by the draugr. But the voices that had woken him, while full of concern and anger, did not have the visceral fear of that night.

When Og-Grim-Dog left their house, it was not hard to find the source of the anguish. The darkness of the night only served to make the burning field a short distance from the foot of their hill more visible. Grim made his way to stand with Hassletoff and Belus at the edge of the hilltop.

'The barley field,' said the halfling despondently. 'There goes our plans for beer next year. I don't know how Raya is going to take this.'

'Just the barley field?' Og asked.

'So far,' said Belus. 'We have to pray to Marduk that it doesn't spread.'

'A fire in the night-time?' Grim asked. 'It must be deliberate. But surely the draugr didn't do this. Has anyone seen movement down there?'

'No. But you're right,' said Hassletoff. 'It indicates that we now have more enemies than the draugr to deal with.' He pulled at his moustache. Just as Grim began to move, the halfling grabbed Dog's arm, somehow reading the minds of the three-headed ogre. 'Don't go down there now. Whoever did this may be waiting in an ambush.'

'But if the fire spreads…' said Dog.

'Then it spreads,' said Hassletoff. 'But we can't afford to lose more lives right now, Og-Grim-Dog.'

Grim sighed. It was hard to argue with that.

✳

The dawn revealed more. Og-Grim-Dog stood with his friends and Belus as they took in the scene below them. The damage had been confined to the one field only: the settlement's other crops seemed untouched by fire. Waiting for them was a group of small figures, perhaps ten in all.

'What are they?' Belus asked, a nervous tone to his voice.

'Goblins,' said Grim.

'Looks like we know who burned the barley field,' added Og.

'They're expecting us to go down there?' asked the monk.

'We're gonna go down there, alright,' said Dog, the prospect of bloody vengeance implied.

'We'll hear what they've got to say before there's any cracking of heads,' Hassletoff warned the ogre. 'You can let us deal with this if you wish,' the halfling said to Belus.

'No,' said the founder of Babylon, with more courage than Grim had expected. 'I need to come too.'

The six of them made their way down the rope ladder to the bottom of the hillfort. Og-Grim-Dog went last. They were becoming more accustomed to the descent but were still the slowest by far. Once they reached the bottom, the newly arrived draugr had already been despatched. The group made their way over to their fields. The goblins were still waiting for them. They were lightly armed, with sharp teeth spilling out of their mouths.

'What's the meaning of this?' Assata asked them, her hand on the hilt of her sword, albeit the weapon remained scabbarded. For now.

'A message,' said one of the goblins, its small, black eyes leering at them. This, Grim felt, was unusually bold behaviour for goblins. True enough, there *were* ten of them. But they were talking to a well-armed group, one of whom was—well—a three-headed ogre. Og-Grim-Dog were used to getting a bit more respect.

'Well, you'd better spit out this message if you want to keep your head on your shoulders,' Grim growled at them.

'We could have burned the whole lot,' said the goblin, gesturing at the rest of Babylon's fields and vegetable patches. 'But we don't want to have to do that. We just want our fair share.'

'Your fair share?' said Borte. 'Your fair share is nothing.'

'Now then, there's no need to be like that. That kind of attitude will see these crops destroyed—and no-one gets nothing if that happens. All we're asking for is a portion of what you produce, and some of the meat and milk from the beasts you've got up there,' he added, pointing up to the top of the hillfort. 'Then we can all live in peace and harmony. Everybody gets fed and nobody gets killed. We've got enough problems with these dead'uns walking about, don't you think?'

'Or,' said Dog, the reasonableness of his voice making him sound somehow even more threatening, 'we could just kill you and keep it all for ourselves.'

'Ah,' said another of the goblins. 'But kill us and twenty more come next. And those'll be the unfriendly types. Like my friend says, best for everyone if you just go along with this new reality. Let your little settlement flourish. Seems to me you've put too much work into it to throw it all away with some misplaced sense of righteousness.'

'You think on it,' said the first goblin. 'We'll be back tomorrow to collect our fair share. I hope for your sakes that it's ready and waiting.'

'And who are we speaking to?' asked Og. 'Is one of you little shits the leader of this racket?'

'I am Grarviaksrurm,' said the first goblin, a sickly smile on his lips.

'I am Grarviaksrurm,' said the second with a toothy grin.

'Grarviaksrurm?' Grim muttered. 'I'm sure that's a name I've heard before...'

'Well,' Og began, 'I don't recall—'

'Hush, Og,' said Grim irritably. 'I'm trying to remember.'

'Until tomorrow, then,' said one of the Grarviaksrurms.

The goblins departed, leaving the six of them standing next to a charred and blackened field.

'That's it!' said Grim, retrieving the information from a far corner of his brain. 'Grarviaksrurm was the name of Gary the goblin. Before he changed it to Gary.'

'Hmm,' said Dog. 'I wonder how Gary the goblin is mixed up in this?'

'What should we do?' Belus asked, seemingly less interested in Gary than Og-Grim-Dog was. 'We could give them what they want, I suppose.'

'Do that,' said Assata, 'and they will keep asking for more and more. They've no intention of living in peace and harmony and all that shit. They're only interested in what they can take from us.'

Belus looked crestfallen. It appeared to Grim that this might be all too much for the human. From seclusion in his monastery, reading his books in tranquillity—to a goblin protection racket. It was a big transition to make, and Grim reckoned that his histories of Gal'azu had not prepared him for everything.

'So, what would you suggest we do?' the monk asked.

'There's only one thing we can do,' said Assata.

*

It was a very risky business, waiting out in the open, in the darkness. Putting their back to the trunk of a broad birch tree offered a little protection. The draugr, drawn to the living by some sense that was clearly not sight, came at them with little warning. Og-Grim-Dog, who could see in the dark as well as anyone else in their little group, were ready to dispatch the creatures as soon as they betrayed their presence. But being on constant alert, reacting to every night-time sound, was draining. The ogre worried for their friends, too. Spread about the fields of Babylon, waiting in ambush, they were too far away to be saved if something went wrong.

Still, Grim admitted, everyone had agreed to the plan. There was a good chance that the goblins would return tonight, to make sure that the people of Babylon were suitably intimidated. It was likely that they had left the meeting with Og-Grim-Dog and his friends feeling that more threats were needed. Perhaps they would come to burn another field—even if the more they destroyed, the less they would get in the end.

Three ogre heads turned at the hoot of an owl from a nearby tree. Except they knew it wasn't really an owl that made the noise—it was Raya Sunshine, and it was a warning.

Grim peered around the tree and tried to listen for goblins. It wasn't easy, with two ogre heads on either side. Mostly all he could hear was the inexplicably loud breathing of Og and Dog.

'There,' said Dog, gesturing with his mace.

Grim looked. He could see small shapes creeping towards the wheat field.

'Wait a little,' his brother added, his wolfish face fixed on his prey. 'The same ten, I reckon,' he said eventually. 'Time to go.'

Grim left their spot under the birch and he made his way, as quietly as he was able, to their targets. He knew that his friends would be doing the same: Hassletoff, Assata and Borte, approaching from different positions so that the goblins would be caught in their trap.

Grunts of surprise erupted ahead, indicating that somebody had spotted someone else, though it was impossible to decipher more than that. Then Grim heard the whistling noise of an arrow before it thudded into a target.

Og-Grim-Dog got within sight range of the goblins, a good half-dozen ahead of them. 'Careful!' he had time to warn his brothers, fearing they might mistake one of their friends for the enemy. Then Og was striking out with his pike, the iron blade at its tip piercing flesh and pushing past bone. Grim got closer, and Dog's mace got involved.

There was Borte, her spear twirling in the air at speed, mesmerising her opponent before she thrust forwards, her body working as one with her weapon in a graceful display. Then Grim could see Assata and Hassletoff: mismatched in height, but working together as they took the blows of the goblins on their shields before countering with slashes and thrusts from their swords.

A sound caught Grim's attention. He turned his head just in time to see a goblin escaping the melee, moving fast—faster than Grim could go. If it got away and called reinforcements, they would be in trouble. As he watched it go, a missile struck the creature full in the chest, with enough force to send the goblin tumbling over onto its back. It lay immobile for some short moments, then desperately tried to struggle up. But it had taken too long. Raya appeared out of the darkness, her pale hair streaming behind her as she ran. She slashed a knife down twice and the goblin moved no longer.

'Drop your weapons,' came Assata's voice, snapping Grim's attention back to the main fight.

Two goblins remained, swords and polearms pointed their way. Raya strode towards them too, an arrow held to the loose string of her bow, but ready to pull and release in seconds.

Outnumbered and outmuscled, the goblins reluctantly did as the barbarian ordered.

'Now then,' Dog said. 'We want taking to your main camp where we will have words with your leader and settle this little disagreement.'

'Not possible,' said one of them. 'We are all Grarviaksrurm. You can tell *me* what you have to say.'

It was quite unlike the normal reaction of goblins, who usually had a healthy sense of self-preservation.

Og sighed. 'Look, whatever brainwashed nonsense your leader has filled you with, we have no time for it. You started this little conflict, so you can have no complaints. Now, if we don't get some sense out of you, you're not going to last much longer.'

The goblin shook his head. 'It is you who won't last much longer. We have tried to be reasonable. This—' he said, gesturing at the dead goblins around him, 'may even be forgiven. Grarviaksrurm is nothing if not forgiving. But continue along this course and you will regret it. Consider that a friendly warning.'

Og-Grim-Dog and his companions looked at one another. Assata gave Dog the nod and the mace came down on the goblin's head, killing him instantly.

'Now then,' said Dog, turning to the last remaining goblin. 'We want—'

'I'll take you to Grarviaksrurm,' said the goblin quickly.

'At last,' said Dog, 'someone is seeing sense.'

TOWARDS A RECKONING

Og-Grim-Dog and his friends wasted no time, setting out for the goblins' camp immediately. Their guide, who insisted his name was Grarviaksrurm, had his hands tied behind him. The end of the rope was gripped firmly by Dog, just in case the goblin was tempted to try something.

Walking somehow felt safer than staying in one place—the shuffling draugr were less likely to catch up to them, though they still had to deal with a few who were in their path. All the same, Grim was relieved to see the sun begin to rise, revealing the creatures well before they stumbled into them. It only took one small mistake for someone to end up with a bite. And that would be it.

Their captive was leading them west. When they stopped for breakfast, Assata insisted that he explain exactly where the camp was.

'There is a cavern network,' the goblin explained, 'roughly equidistant between Mer Khazer, Darkspike Dungeon and the border with Magidu. Grarviaksrurm has named it Strong Club.'

'We know it well,' said Grim. 'Uninhabited last I heard,' he added, looking at the goblin with suspicion.

'It was too close to Mer Khazer and all those adventurers to be used as a permanent base in the past,' the captive explained. The goblin allowed himself a smug, toothy smile. 'But times have changed.'

For all the sour looks directed at him, it was hard to argue. Mer Khazer was overrun; its people scattered; the Bureau finished. New powers were already beginning to take its place. Grim pondered on it. Who would come out on top? Communities like Babylon, or brigands like these goblins?

Still, knowing their destination filled Grim and his friends with a bit more confidence; gave them a greater sense of control. Until, that was, they looked down on the bridge that spanned the River Trib as it flowed south-west to the ocean. Grim could see the beginnings of the cavern network where Grarviaksrurm had made his headquarters on the opposite bank. It was a rocky land that the river had carved through, leaving a deep chasm that the wood and rope bridge traversed.

But there was a problem. The bridge was packed solid with draugr, hundreds of them. It swung alarmingly. The latest arrivals were not even able to reach the bridge—their path blocked by the solid wall of their brethren, they pushed and moaned, seemingly with inexhaustible patience.

Raya pointed to a metal cage that had been hung in the centre of the bridge. 'There's someone in there—a human male, I think. They're attracting the draugr.'

'Too many to get through,' said Hassletoff dolefully.

'The bridge isn't even safe,' Assata added. 'It could collapse at any moment, and that's some drop.'

'Your leader did this?' Og asked their captive. 'To block this route into the caverns?'

The goblin shrugged. 'The bridge was free when I was last here. But yes, it must have been Grarviaksrurm.'

'Why would he do it?'

The goblin shrugged.

'I don't like this,' Og muttered.

'What is it, Og?' Borte asked him.

'I have a bad feeling that they know we're coming.'

'It's not too late to take a step back,' the goblin suggested. 'A bit of compromise on your part could avoid a lot of unpleasantness.'

'That ain't gonna happen,' said Dog.

'There's another way to the caverns,' Grim offered. 'It means backtracking then circling around. It'll add at least a day to the journey.'

They looked at one another. It seemed to be the only option on the table—bar giving up and returning to Babylon; or giving in to the goblins' demands. It was, therefore, the only option they could stomach.

'Lead on, then, Og-Grim-Dog,' said Hassletoff.

✳

They were lucky to spot a nobleman's hunting lodge before nightfall. It had a cleared area around it, surrounded by ditches and an earthen bank. The wooden walls were sturdy, and it was plenty big enough for their party. Inside, it seemed untouched: the equipment for hunting, preparing and cooking remained, as well as blankets and various items of clothing, suggesting that the lodge was unoccupied when the sickness hit the region.

Despite the security offered by the lodge, a rota for night watch was agreed. An eye had to be kept on their captive, as well as any draugr attracted by their presence.

Og-Grim-Dog took first watch. The goblin, trussed up for the night, soon went to sleep. Or at least, it did a very good impression of sleeping, since it was soon snoring.

The draugr began to arrive about halfway through the ogre's watch. Grim could hear them outside, navigating their way clumsily across the ditches outside, moaning in their eternal quest for living flesh. When they reached the walls of the lodge, they began to smash their limbs against the walls. The door rattled alarmingly, and Og-Grim-Dog pushed some of the furniture up against it to keep the weak point secure.

A plank of wood at the front of the lodge cracked, and then burst inwards. An arm, bones visible beneath the decaying flesh, pushed through the gap. Its hand grasped open and closed, in a vain attempt to clutch at those inside the lodge.

Og-Grim-Dog's friends woke at the noise, staring groggily at the sight of an arm poking into their abode, and the pile of furniture in front of the door.

Raya sighed. She rubbed at her eyes and Grim wondered if he saw a wetness of tears there, quickly wiped away. 'I'm not getting back to sleep with this racket going on. I'll take my watch now.'

'I'll join you,' said Hassletoff.

Grim settled down. True enough, it wasn't ideal conditions for sleeping. But Og-Grim-Dog had lived beneath a clan of kobolds for several years, and a fitful sleep soon took them.

Og-Grim-Dog awoke to find that Assata and Borte had prepared a meal from the provisions they carried and those they had found in the lodge. It wasn't exactly the equal of the fare at The Dark Lord's refectory: but it supplied them with enough energy to face the day ahead. For today, surely, there would be the reckoning with the goblins.

Outside, the lodge was now fully surrounded by draugr, and that was the topic of conversation over breakfast.

'We don't want to be swinging weapons in here,' said Assata. 'Too likely to cause an accident.'

'Then we smash our way through the back wall,' Grim offered. 'The rest of you follow up, take out the immediate threats. Then we outpace the rest.'

The others nodded their agreement. It was the safest option, though Og-Grim-Dog would be risking a bite as they broke through.

'What about me?' whined the goblin. 'I can't outpace them tied up like this.'

It was met with a mix of reluctant and suspicious expressions. Still, Grim supposed, the creature had a point.

'I'll cut you free,' said Raya at last. 'But any attempt to escape and my retribution will be swift.'

She drew a knife and cut through the ropes that bound the creature.

'We should make some noise at the front of the house,' suggested Borte. 'Draw some of them away.'

'Good idea,' said Hassletoff. 'Everyone ready?'

They banged fists and the hilts of weapons against the internal walls of the lodge, while the draugr continued to bash from the other side. They stopped, listening to see if their actions had made a difference. Grim thought he might have detected the sound of movement from outside, but it was near impossible to tell amidst the moans of the draugr.

'Once more,' Raya ordered, and Og-Grim-Dog's friends made yet more noise as Grim readied himself for the charge. He put one foot behind him against the front wall of the lodge, poised not very far from the draugr arm that still grabbed at thin air through the hole that it had made.

'Ready?' he asked.

'Ready,' came the reply.

Grim pushed off from the wall and ran the short distance towards the opposite end of the lodge. He twisted, sending Dog's shoulder into the wall. With a crack, it gave way as the ogre's bulk smashed into it. Grim tried to keep his feet, but as he barrelled through the wooden planks, he tripped over something substantial, and went flying forwards, landing hard on the ground outside the lodge.

Grim struggled on the ground, trying to co-ordinate with Og and Dog who had to push up their heavy torso with their hands. He heard the moans of the draugr about him, then he found himself tipping forwards. His face hit the ground, giving him a mouthful of dirt.

Grim leg's scrabbled about until he was able to get first one knee, then the other onto the ground. Once Og-Grim-Dog had heaved themselves up into a kneeling position, Grim was able to get one foot down and push up into a standing position.

He found himself inside a protective circle. His friends lashed out with swords and spear, hacking into any draugr that got too close. Grim wasted no more time in moving away from the lodge, getting to a safer distance from the creatures. His friends followed his lead, as the draugr from the front of the lodge began to emerge around the side.

Grim watched as Raya dropped her sword to the ground and grabbed her bow, then an arrow. As she fitted the missile to the string and aimed, all in one fluid motion, he saw what she had seen. Some distance away already, their captured goblin was sprinting off in another direction. The arrow arced up and down, finding its mark as it felled the goblin.

The goblin writhed on the ground, yelling in pain, before it struggled to its feet. The arrow had found the back of its leg. As it tried to hobble away, it collapsed back to the ground, producing fresh screams of agony. All of which attracted more than a few of the draugr, who were now staggering towards the injured creature.

'Help!' it yelled, getting to its feet once more. 'Help me!'

'It occurs to me,' said Grim, 'that we don't really need him now that we know where Grarviaksrurm's camp is located.'

'I told him retribution would be swift,' Raya reminded them as she retrieved her sword and they began to vacate the scene.

Except, the retribution wasn't so swift—since Grim could hear the goblin's screams for quite some time afterwards.

STRONG CLUB

It was a good couple of hours walking until Og-Grim-Dog led the group to the alternative crossing of the River Trib. Huge stepping stones stretched from one bank to the other.

'It is said that ogres laid the stones here,' said Dog proudly. It was hardly architecture that compared to the imperial palace in Pengshui or the Dark Lord's fortress of Fell Towers—but everyone was kind enough to make impressed noises.

The ogre's friends looked up and down river, wary of any traps or obstacles placed here by Grarviaksrurm and his goblins, like the one across the bridge yesterday.

'Can't see anything,' said Raya at last, after some careful observation.

'The draugr would find it hard to keep their balance on those stones,' said Dog, gesturing at the irregular shapes in the river.

They glistened wetly from the constant splash of the water. Losing one's balance on such a slippery surface would almost certainly result in a dunking. Grim was doubtful that a draugr, once caught in the river's current, would be able to save itself from getting carried downriver.

'Speaking of which,' said Og, 'Director Hassletoff. May we offer you transport across the river?'

The gaps between the stones were indeed too wide for someone of a halfling's stature. Grim was pleased that his brother had made the suggestion so politely.

Assata led them across the stones, her sword drawn just in case there was an unseen ambush waiting for them. Grim followed behind Borte, his brothers carrying Hassletoff in a comfortable looking seated position. Grim wasn't the most agile of creatures, but his weight leant a certain advantage on this occasion. Once he placed a foot down, it took quite a lot to shift it.

Raya was the last to cross. When she joined them on the far bank, the elf looked about the rocky terrain once more. A slight frown played on her features as she studied their location. Thick woodland stretched to the north-east, while the cavernous rocks where Grarviaksrurm had made his headquarters lay to the south-west. With a little shrug, she gave the all clear to continue.

The ground beneath their feet became hard rock. Walls of natural stone rose about them, while the dark maws of cave entrances began to appear, increasingly frequent, at various heights and angles in the landscape. All of them too small, or too inaccessible, for their needs.

While a dark, dank grotto was an appealing sight to an ogre, Grim noticed that his companions grew more tense the farther they entered this terrain. Raya seemed particularly suspicious, her bow in one hand, the other never far from her quiver of arrows.

'We'll get a little farther,' Grim said quietly, in an attempt to reassure his friends. 'Then use the first large entrance we find.'

It was just as Grim was saying these words, one eye on his elven friend, that he noticed her eyes suddenly snap wide. An arrow appeared in her spare hand and she was turning, pulling back the string of her weapon.

Grim turned to look in the direction she was aiming, as the word 'Enemy!' left her mouth.

Goblins. Pouring out of one opening; then the next. They jumped out from high tunnels onto the rocky ground, moving swiftly to their targets. Others came running around corners—from all directions. Hundreds appeared, and yet more kept coming, surrounding them. Raya had released her first arrow and put a second to her string. But she stopped. Grim had to agree that doing any more seemed pointless.

The goblins surrounded them, keeping their distance. They grinned; they leered; they waved their crude weapons at the trespassers in their midst; but they refrained from attacking, even though they could have overwhelmed Og-Grim-Dog and his friends in short measure.

Then, something else came. Grim saw it approach, even before the crowd of goblins parted before it. A one-headed ogre. He was significantly taller than Og-Grim-Dog, with bulging muscles on his bare torso, arms and legs. A massive club hung on his belt. Riding on one shoulder was Grarviaksrurm, once known as Gary the goblin.

'Og-Grim-Dog,' said the ogre, nodding solemnly in their direction.

'Megrok the Slayer,' Dog acknowledged. It had been a while since Og-Grim-Dog had seen another ogre. They tended to avoid one another. 'What are you doing here?' Dog asked, his tone friendly enough given the circumstances.

'These damned dead things—forced me to leave my territory. It's an altogether more congenial atmosphere here.'

'Lower me down,' Gary ordered Megrok, who obliged by depositing the goblin leader on the ground. 'Let's get our visitors tied up,' he instructed his followers, before turning to Og-Grim-Dog and his companions. 'Drop your weapons.'

'And if we don't?' Assata asked.

The goblins went silent, staring from Assata to their leader, creating a hush of anticipation.

'That's a rather silly question,' Gary said quietly into the silence. 'I won't ask a second time.'

'We fail Sandon if we all fall here,' said Raya, putting down her bow and quiver, then unbuckling her sword belt.

Reluctantly, her friends followed her lead.

As soon as they dropped their weapons, the goblins were onto them, forcing them to the ground, ropes tied about hands and feet. Grim wondered whether fighting it out might have been the better option. Megrok the Slayer came for Og-Grim-Dog, with a special length of rope thick enough to secure them. They knew full well that the ogre would have no compunction in striking them dead if he felt like it. So Grim got to his knees, while Og and Dog offered up their wrists, hands clasped together.

'In a row,' ordered Gary.

Og-Grim-Dog's friends were dragged next to them, goblins grabbing at hair as well as limbs and throwing them down roughly. Dog gave a deep warning growl, but it was too late to fight now. They had chosen to take whatever punishment the goblin was about to mete out.

When he had them kneeling in a row just as he liked, the goblin began.

'So, you came here to kill me?' he asked them. 'Why is that always the first reaction you people have to goblins? We could have worked together; built an alliance. Instead, we have this unpleasantness.'

'You sent your people to take from us,' said Assata.

'To protect Babylon, you mean. We only asked for a small portion of what you were growing. We need to eat as well, you know. Was that such a high price to pay? I didn't think so. But your instincts took over your sense, correct? You saw goblins and refused us. You saw goblins and killed them, then marched here to exterminate us.'

'Oh please,' said Borte, 'spare us the self-pity. You started all this.'

Gary gave a bitter laugh. 'My soldiers had instructions not to kill. Are you telling me they ignored my orders?'

Borte said nothing.

'And where are they?' the goblin leader asked. 'All dead, right? Still, I'm sure you all shed a tear over the dead goblins. One survived though? You made him take you here, no? Where is he, I wonder?' Gary asked, making a show of looking around for the goblin that Raya had shot down.

'How do you know all that?' asked Og.

He smiled and clicked his fingers. A figure was shoved forwards through the crowd of goblins. It was Belus.

'Belus here saw sense. Warned me that you were coming.'

'You fucking traitor,' said Assata.

Belus looked offended. 'I have a community to protect. Civilisation must continue. That means taking tough decisions. You were...too quick to resort to violence.'

'A community in thrall to a pack of greenskins?' Dog spat out. 'Good luck with that.'

'Oh, it's all coming out now, isn't it?' said Gary, looking about at his followers. 'The racial slurs. These races have always thought us beneath them, haven't they?' His goblin followers nodded and called out their agreement. 'Sub-humans. Greenskins. Army fodder for every sociopathic warlord trying to tear down civilization. An unwanted pestilence that the so-called civilized races need to eradicate. Hunted; persecuted; enslaved.'

'I'm not disagreeing with you,' Og offered. 'But you were building your way out of that subservient role you had been cast in.

You changed your name to Gary. You established a postal service. What happened?'

Gary shook his head at Grim's brother. 'You don't get it? I thought more of you, Og,' he added, sounding disappointed. 'I was trying to fit in to the human's world. Taking a human name, starting up a business. But it was still a subservient business, wasn't it? Carrying important people's letters for them. But that world has gone now. The undead monsters have destroyed it. A new world is coming. A world where goblins can thrive.

'Smaller and weaker than some. More stupid and ugly than others. We didn't stand a chance before. But this is a world that suits us just fine. In a world where food is scarce it pays to be scrawny—to be able to get by on scraps. What use is reading and education and great magic and high morals in this world? Who is there to make fine armour? To supply great armies? To devote time and resources in creating mighty warriors or wizards? This is a world where people will betray their lofty principles to steal some crusts from their neighbours. And do it again the next day, and the next. This is a world made for the monstrous and the grotesque.'

Gary pointed at his prisoners. 'That's a lesson you are yet to learn. But I'm going to teach it now. Those I let live will have the chance to apply the lesson to the remainder of their lives.'

He held out one arm and one of his followers handed him a club. It was as plain and ordinary a looking weapon as one might ever see, and yet it filled Grim with a sense of fear and dread.

'Don't do this,' Grim said. It was part plea and part warning. He could tell that Gary didn't care for it.

'Did it cross your mind, even once, to spare *our* friends? To give *them* a second chance?'

Grim hung his head. There was no point in lying about it.

'I could use one such as you,' Gary said, gesturing at Og-Grim-Dog with his club, 'if you are willing to change course. For that reason, you are spared today.'

That was a blow more painful than if Megrok had been ordered to crack Grim over the head. Because it meant that one of his friends would suffer instead.

'Halflings, however, have no place in this world.'

The goblin's club came down on Hassletoff's head. Once, twice, and more, until there was nothing left that could be called a head. The goblins that circled them cackled and capered as the tension of the encounter was finally released.

A deep fire began in Grim's bowels, spreading through his body. His legs tingled with it and his body began to move of its own accord.

'Steady,' said Megrok, his hands firm on Og-Grim-Dog's shoulders, keeping Grim on his knees. 'Now is not your time.'

Dog bit his arm and Megrok withdrew his hands with a yelp, then put them around the handle of his giant club. He hefted it, ready to bring it down. Grim knew there would be no more warnings from Megrok the Slayer.

Gary strutted about, hands held out wide, gore dripping from the end of his club. He took in the adulation of his followers, sharing their triumphant grins. For all his self-righteous words, this was what his kind had always sought. The power of life and death over their victims.

'Neither,' he said, his voice rising to an exultation, as if this had become a sacrificial rite, 'do elvenkind.'

'No!' shouted Og-Grim-Dog.

The club came down on Raya.

Grim found himself lurching to his feet, the rope tied about his legs bursting open. Og and Dog ripped apart their bonds.

But that was as far as they got, as a great force pummelled them. Dog's head thudded into the right side of Grim's head. Grim's neck was jerked to the side, his head ricocheting against Og's and back again. His legs turned to jelly, and he felt himself collapse to the ground. Grim's vision swam in front of him. He tasted blood in his mouth and a queasy sensation filled his guts. He thought he could hear the cries of Assata and Borte through the ringing in his ears.

Then the world turned black.

REVELATIONS

Grim woke with a sore head, a sickly stomach and a broken heart.

Dog was groaning and Og was telling him to shut up. This explained why he was awake. It also told him that his brothers were alive. But as the memories of what Gary the goblin had done washed back into his consciousness, the images of Hassletoff and Raya's final moments returned to his mind, and Grim wished he hadn't woken up at all.

Og-Grim-Dog sat up and looked about. They were at the bottom of a rocky slope. Judging by the scrapes and grazes on their limbs, they had likely been rolled down the slope. For whatever reason, Gary had seen fit to eject them from his camp, rather than killing them.

That might prove to be a mistake on his part.

A few feet away, two figures huddled over a small fire. Assata and Borte turned to look at the ogre. Their faces were full of sorrow—and a second emotion, that Grim couldn't quite identify.

'What happened?' Grim asked, his voice coming out as a dry croak.

Borte brought over a pot of water and the three heads each drank thirstily until it was empty.

'That ogre hit you pretty hard,' said Assata when they were done. 'You blacked out. I thought you might be dead,' she added, as if that would have been a source of regret, which Grim appreciated. 'They let us go, with instructions to head back to Babylon. Gary wants us to prepare for another goblin acquisition party. They're coming for double what they asked for before. Another lesson from Grarviaksrurm.'

Og-Grim-Dog managed to get to their feet, stagger their way to the fire and sit down again. Grim's head spun and he felt like he was going to be sick.

'We're not intending to give them what they want, are we?' Dog growled. 'That's hardly what Raya and Hassletoff would have wanted.'

Assata and Borte exchanged a look.

'What is it?' Og demanded. 'You've been acting like you've some great secret to share for a while now. Why don't you just come on out with it?'

'Alright. All this is our fault,' Assata said, a strange tone to her voice.

Grim wasn't at all sure what the barbarian was talking about. Did she mean the death of their friends at the hands of the former postgoblin, Gary? Or something else?

'All what?' he demanded.

'Remember the retreat from Kuthenia to Mer Khazer?' said Borte. 'We were full of anger at the decision.'

'Me especially,' Assata admitted. 'Then you, Sandon and Raya went off on your quest to Varena. I was left seething with anger. And I fell victim to fear—that the Kuthenians would come and destroy us. Those people who had risked everything for our cause, would be left defenceless. So, I resolved to do something about it. I decided to ask Nick to help—'

'Nick Romancer?' asked Dog in a perplexed voice. 'What did you think *he* was going to do?'

'*We* went to see him,' Borte corrected. 'It was a joint decision. We asked him to use his skills to devise a weapon that could stop the Kuthenians in their tracks. To save us—at least for a while. Nick came up with the idea of the draugr. He brewed a potion, designed to infect its victim with a sickness that would reanimate their body after death. While you went on your adventures to Varena and the Pirate Isles, Assata, Nick and I went on ours. We snuck out of Mer Khazer—we didn't tell Toff, or anyone else. And we took Nick's potion into Kuthenia.'

Grim's mind was reeling. 'So, when you say all this was your fault, you really do mean, *all* this.' This was a moment when Grim wished he had a pair of hands to visually encompass the scale of what they had done. It wasn't just the deaths of their friends, painful and raw as that was. It was the death of thousands of humans and other creatures; the destruction of countless towns and cities—the end of civilisation. Grim was an ogre, well used to ending individual lives. He had even participated in a brutal war of attrition against the Kuthenians that had seen hundreds of deaths with every pitched battle. But the extent of devastation wrought by Nick's weapon was hard to fathom.

'It wasn't our intention,' said Assata. 'I'm not trying to excuse what I've done, and I'll answer for it in Gehenna, no doubt. My goal was to weaken the Kuthenians—to occupy them with another enemy. But the sickness was more virulent than we thought possible. And it wasn't long before the draugr began to spread into the territory of The Free Cities. As soon as we realised what was happening, Nick began work on an elixir, to remedy the effects of his potion. That's why we stayed in Mer Khazer for so long, in the hope that he would find the correct formula. Of course, he never did.'

'Hassletoff knew by that point?' Og asked.

'We told him,' said Borte. 'He stayed to help us, just as you would expect him to.'

Tears came to the princess's eyes at the thought of their dead friend.

'What now?' asked Assata. 'I'm sure none of us feel like returning to Babylon. Sandon and Raya wanted us to deal with Lilith and Samael—they always considered them to be the real threat. Perhaps the biggest damage I have done is allowed our attention to be diverted elsewhere. Maybe we should leave this mess behind.'

'If you decide you don't want to work with us anymore, Og-Grim-Dog,' Borte added, 'we will understand. If you were to crush our skulls in right now, I wouldn't argue either.'

'Hardly,' said Dog. 'Lilith and Samael need to be dealt with, that's true enough. But Og-Grim-Dog doesn't walk away when they have friends who need to be avenged.'

'And,' said Grim, his mind still ticking over, 'I have an idea about how we might achieve that.'

THE ONLY THING WORSE THAN TROLLS

There was little in the way of conversation as they travelled south-east from the goblin camp. They moved fast, outpacing the draugr that still roamed the Great Outside. There was something about watching your friends die that left the usual necessities of life unnecessary: food, or resting, for example. Instead they walked with a relentless kind of energy, fuelled by bitterness and loss.

Og-Grim-Dog found themselves thinking more than they were used to. Grim's mind switched from recent events; to the revelations from Assata and Borte; to the long-term goal of defeating the succubus, Lilith. In the end, his thoughts always returned to the image of Gary, a club, and his friend Raya, and he knew that he wouldn't find any peace until he got his revenge—or died trying.

When Grim studied them, he suspected that Assata and Borte felt a little better after unburdening themselves of their role in the apocalypse. Whether they deserved to, he just couldn't decide. All these thoughts jostling around in his head made his brain hurt. He looked forward to the end of the day when sleep would give him a respite from the incessant rumination. But sleep was elusive.

There was, therefore, a sense of relief when their destination came into view. If nothing else, it offered a chance for the ogre to do something, rather than simply stew over what had happened.

It had been a while since Og-Grim-Dog had seen the rocky exterior of Darkspike Dungeon. The place seemed so much smaller now: perhaps because the world had turned out to be so much larger than they had realized.

'I know it probably goes without saying,' said Og. 'But let us do the talking.'

'Don't worry,' said Borte. 'This is my first time in a dungeon. I'll follow your lead.'

They entered unchallenged. Grim led them through the guardroom. Normally filled with goblins, it lay empty.

'I presume,' said Grim, 'that the goblins of Darkspike have all gone over to Strong Club.'

'But we still need to be ready,' warned Dog.

Indeed, once they had passed through the guardroom and begun to take the sloping corridor that led into the heart of Darkspike, they were soon challenged.

'What are you doing here?' came a voice from the darkness.

Two figures emerged, both gripping spears aimed at Og-Grim-Dog. Taller and broader than their goblin cousins, orcs were dangerous. Grim assumed that the only reason they hadn't already attacked, was that they recognised the ogre as a former resident here; or at least as a former ally in the war in Kuthenia.

'We've come to see your queen,' Grim explained.

'You've brought humans here?' one of them asked, a snarl coming to its face.

Violence seemed imminent, and that would do them no good.

'They're here to see Krim, too,' said Dog, keeping the tone of his voice casual. 'I suggest you let her decide whether they're welcome or not.'

Crossing the Queen of the Orcs wasn't good for one's health, and hesitation came to the faces of the two orcs.

'Alright,' one of them relented at last. 'We will take you to see the queen.' He allowed himself a smile. 'Maybe then we'll kill you.'

'Her Exalted Royal Majesty, Sovereign and Despot of the Black Orcs of Darkspike Dungeon, Overlord of the Orc Nation!' declared Krim's standard-bearer grandly.

Dog rolled his eyes but wisely kept his opinions to himself. They really needed this meeting to go well.

Krim had a throne room set up, not so dissimilar in appearance to the one that belonged to The Dark Lord. Her orc warriors lounged about, lacking the discipline of the menials of Fell Towers. They looked at the three arrivals hungrily, hoping that their queen would give the order to tear the trespassers to pieces. There were at least twenty of them in this room alone, many more spread out along this level of the dungeon. If such an order was given, Og-Grim-Dog and his friends wouldn't stand a chance.

Borte knelt before Queen Krim. The motion took Grim and Assata by surprise, but with some reluctance they followed her lead.

'You may rise,' said Krim, looking pleased with the gesture of subservience. She lounged on her carved wooden throne, one leg lazily sprawled over an arm of the chair, her black eyes glittering with intelligence. 'To what do I owe this pleasure? Let me guess. Your forces are destroyed by the draugr and you come seeking refuge here?'

'Sort of,' said Og. 'Our forces *are* destroyed. Our friends are dead, save for those you see here.' If Og had hoped such news would illicit some sympathy, he was disappointed. Krim looked on, waiting for him to get to the point. 'But the draugr weren't responsible for all those deaths. We fell foul of Grarviaksrurm.'

'Ah. That little sack of shit. Bad luck. But what's all this tragedy got to do with me?'

'Those goblins in Strong Club are a threat to you. Grarviaksrurm is only getting more powerful. We've witnessed him subduing one community to his rule. There may already be others, and if not, more will come eventually. If you don't act now, he will expand across this part of Gal'azu and you will have lost your chance.'

'What community?' Krim asked suspiciously.

'Babylon,' Assata confirmed.

'Never heard of it.'

'We were there,' said the barbarian, in a tone that left little doubt.

'Pah,' said the queen. 'You've failed to deal with the goblins, and you've come to get us to do it. We're not your servants, for you to order about!'

Krim's orcs snarled and growled at these words.

'You promised us a kingdom in Gal'azu and all we got were dead orcs and a lost war.'

The orc warriors brandished their weapons. They waited only for the order to finish these trespassers.

'You'll have our help to defeat the goblins,' said Dog.

'Your help?' Krim gestured at them. 'You really think the three of you can swing the outcome?'

The orcs laughed and smirked along with their leader.

'They have an ogre,' said Dog. 'You'll need our help to deal with it.'

'I *know* they have an ogre,' said Krim. 'I know about the goblins' dispositions. I'm not a complete idiot. I also know that if we launch an attack on Strong Club, many more orcs will die. Even if we win, we'll be left weakened. Why should I take such a risk?'

'This is your chance,' Grim offered. 'With Grarviaksrurm dead, there'll be no-one left to stop you building your kingdom. Well, no-one living, anyway. You'll still have the draugr to deal with. But no-one else in this part of Gal'azu can raise an army to match what you have. Maybe you'll be weakened, but you'll be victorious.' Grim paused, searching for the right words. 'Then, perhaps, your standard bearer will introduce you as Queen Krim the Great.'

Krim snorted with derision, as if such titles were beneath her.

But Grim knew otherwise.

She eyed them slyly as she considered her options.

'Things haven't been easy here, you know,' she said finally. 'The illness hasn't spared us, if that's what you were thinking. I've had to be ruthless, in killing anyone with signs of infection. But we have a serious problem down below. The infection reached the trolls and they were too stupid to stop it. They're totally wiped out and only two things remain.'

'What do you mean…things?' asked Og.

'Draugr trolls, of course.' Krim gave them her sly look again. 'Here's the deal on offer. Get rid of them for us, and we'll join with you and crush Grarviaksrurm.'

The orc warriors cheered and clashed their weapons, as ready to kill goblins as they were for the three trespassers to be slaughtered by undead trolls.

Grim sighed. They had little choice but to accept.

'Trolls,' muttered Dog. 'The only thing worse than trolls, are undead trolls.'

A VERY UNPLEASANT SMELL

Og-Grim-Dog, Assata and Borte made their way down to the next level of Darkspike Dungeon. They didn't make any attempt to move stealthily, as adventurers might ordinarily have done. They had learned that the draugr could sense the living, with an ability beyond that of sight or of hearing. It therefore did little good to move slowly, or quietly, or keep to the dark. Far better to arrive, they had decided, with some element of surprise.

They came alone, Krim not deigning to send any of her warriors with them. Grim knew that if the three of them died down here, the orc queen wouldn't mind one bit. She would take it as a cue to stay holed up in the dungeon and not risk a showdown with Gary and his goblins. Grim also knew that the odds of them dying down here were high. Still, they hadn't seriously considered turning down Krim's offer. They were too committed to this course of action to turn aside at the last moment.

As the slope levelled off and they found themselves in the trolls' lair, an eye-wateringly unpleasant smell hit them. Even the two humans smelt it, both struggling not to bring up the contents of their stomachs. Trolls smelt bad enough—as did draugr. The combination of the two was appalling.

Getting the scent of their quarry was one thing. Identifying where it was coming from was another. Fortunately, Dog's nose was an olfactory organ par excellence.

'Take the left corridor,' he instructed Grim, who followed his brother's directions, turning one way then the next. Sure enough, the smell grew even stronger. It led them to an underground chamber. It was spacious; circular; with other corridors running off it. Scattered about the hall were the dismembered, half-eaten corpses of several orcs—no doubt Krim's warriors who had failed to neutralise this unique enemy. Standing in amongst the bones were two trolls. They groaned—a resonant, repulsive sound that was part troll and part draugr. Each clutched a weapon—the huge clubs favoured by their kind. It was rare to find draugr using weapons, Grim noted. Perhaps the sickness concocted by Nick Romancer affected trolls in some subtly different way.

'How odd,' said Dog, as the two trolls staggered towards them, their faces vacant, even for trolls. 'I'm sure we've seen these two fellows before.'

'I don't recall meeting them before,' Og countered.

But Grim did. Over the next few seconds, his mind functioned at maximum speed, as he analysed the situation. They had come across these ogres twice, both times in Varena. Perhaps it was the draugr that had chased the trolls this far south. The first run in had come while on The Dark Lord's business, on their way to kill Karlens Stone in Yeggton. The second time had been in the company of Sandon and Raya, on their journey from Mer Khazer to the Oracle of Britrona. On both occasions there had been three of them—brothers, he had guessed.

Three of them.

Grim spun around, calling out a warning.

Sure enough, the third troll had crept up from behind and was almost on them, its club already raised for a strike. Og launched his pike. It flew true and with power, slamming into the troll and piercing its thick hide. The impact sent it flailing backwards, crashing to the dungeon floor, the pole still embedded in its torso.

It was Assata who gave the next warning. The other two trolls were on them now, suddenly moving much faster. But Grim had no time to wonder at the ability of these undead to deceive and ambush.

For Og-Grim-Dog now found themselves in one of the most desperate fights of their life.

In a blur of frenetic activity, spear, sword and clubs struck out in a brutal melee. Grim tried to avoid the great swinging clubs of the trolls while manoeuvring Dog into position to strike with his mace. He was half successful. Dog got a good hit in, breaking troll skull. But a club thudded into Og's shoulder, spinning the ogre about until they crashed into the wall. Panicking—cursing his clumsiness—Grim desperately tried to get upright, his brothers pushing up from floor and wall.

Back on their feet, Og-Grim-Dog only had moments to brace themselves for the impact from the troll that Og had sent sprawling. Ordinarily, his thrown pike might have done enough damage to keep the troll down. But this was a draugr, and such injuries seemed meaningless to the undead. Og managed to get a grip around the neck of their attacker before the troll's momentum sent them crashing to the floor, landing heavily on their back. Dog's mace fell from his grip, while the troll had landed on top of them— Og's grip around its neck the only thing preventing it from catching Grim's nose in its powerful jaw. Even so, the stink from its foul breath was nearly enough to finish Grim off.

Dog put his hand to the other side of the troll's neck and was able to push it away a few inches. But with the troll on top of them, Og-Grim-Dog were unable to push it off—and it wasn't possible to strangle a draugr.

Just as Grim considered the prospect that his final moments would be spent trapped underneath an undead troll, the tip of a sword blade emerged through the middle of its face, while dead troll gore spattered Grim's. He closed his eyes to protect them from the liquid and waited for what seemed like an inordinate amount of time for his brothers to heave the troll off.

'Wipe my face,' he asked, as they got up to a sitting position.

Grim simply wasn't expecting the sight that greeted him when he opened his eyes. Two of the three troll brothers lay dead around them. But so did Borte. It was clear that a troll club had caught her, and her fragile body hadn't been able to withstand such a blow.

Assata had her sword aimed at the third troll. It was pinned to the wall of the dungeon by spear and pike, that had pierced its limbs. Still, it struggled mightily, jaw snapping, threatening to break free. Assata's sword arm shook.

'Kill it!' Og warned her, as Grim struggled to his feet.

'I have a better idea,' said the barbarian, her voice the sound of steel striking against granite. 'If you could subdue it for me.'

Grim marched over and Dog gripped the scalp of the troll, driving its head into the wall.

Assata let her sword drop to the floor of the dungeon with a clang. She sat beside the Kuthenian princess and began to stroke her dark hair. A haunted look came to the barbarian's face as she whispered words that no-one else could hear.

✶

Assata insisted on carrying Borte's body all the way to the orcs' throne room herself. When she laid the corpse down on the floor, Queen Krim at least had the good grace to look a little shame faced.

Og-Grim-Dog laid a second body on the floor. An undead troll, tied up with rope, one of the ogre's hemp sacks secured over its head.

'It is done,' said Dog, his voice a mix of sorrow and anger.

The Overlord of the Orc Nation nodded in acknowledgement. 'Then I will honour our agreement. The Black Orcs of Darkspike Dungeon will go to war against the goblins.'

SHOWDOWN

K rim insisted that they wait until night to launch their attack. Og-Grim-Dog and Assata gave way to her greater knowledge of goblin behaviour; besides, she was the one with the army.

The orc leader also insisted they march straight for Grarviaksrurm's camp by the direct route.

'It will give his scouts less chance to see us coming,' she explained.

'There was a problem with the bridge when we went that way,' said Og. 'Full of draugr. Gary has put up a metal cage with a human inside to attract them and block passage.'

'Pretty ruthless,' said Krim, sounding impressed. 'Let's see what we see, shall we?'

When they got there, they found that they were in luck. The draugr had disappeared.

'It may be unstable,' Assata warned.

'Not convinced it'll take our weight,' Dog agreed, patting the troll he was carrying over his shoulder. The troll moaned in response—something pitiful in the noise to Grim's ears.

'Not to worry,' said Krim.

She had a few hundred soldiers at her disposal and once they had their orders, they moved quickly. Trees were soon being felled, timber stripped, and logs hauled to the site of the bridge. The orcs took care when laying them along the bridge, avoiding placing too much weight onto the structure until the new logs were lashed in place. When done, they provided a stronger platform for their army to march across. Grim couldn't help but be impressed with the no-nonsense orc engineering on display.

They crossed the river. Half way along, Grim got sight of the reason why the draugr had dispersed. The human in the cage had died. A draugr now moaned at them as the orc army marched past its prison, fruitlessly banging at the metal bars in its desperation to satiate its new hunger.

✶

Grim collapsed on the top of the crag, as his brothers finally released their hold on the huge burden that was the draugr troll. Being dead didn't seem to have reduced its weight appreciably and the strain of dragging it up to this height had almost been too much. Og-Grim-Dog lay gasping for breath, utterly spent, trying their utmost not to make a sound that would give their presence away to the goblins beneath them.

They allowed smaller, more nimble fingers, to prepare the troll for its descent. Once secured with ropes, they began the process of lowering the monster down the crevice that Krim had identified. Og-Grim-Dog had recovered enough to help. Their strength at the end of the rope helped to keep it steady, despite the troll beginning to move more freely. Assata had suggested that they partially cut through some ropes, and loosen others, so that it was able to free itself when it reached the bottom.

The sack that covered its head was removed at the last moment. The troll disappeared from view as the rope was lowered further, groans echoing back up to the surface as it went. Grim feared that the noise would draw the goblins. But the weight on the rope disappeared—the troll had landed—and still there was no alarm raised from the goblins.

'They've got a surprise coming their way,' said Dog.

Grim had to smile in agreement. The idea of a draugr troll running amok in Gary's camp was indeed something to be savoured.

They looked at one another in the moonlight, waiting for the sound of a reaction down below. They all knew this was a mighty risk: an all-or-nothing gamble that they could overcome Gary's forces. If not, they would die here. Krim seemed content enough with her decision. Assata appeared to be ready to give her life. The barbarian was not someone given to outward emotions, but Grim had noticed that she carried a certain fatalism about her—ever since the death of Princess Borte.

'Og,' Grim prompted.

'Oh yes,' said Og, rummaging about in his belt bag. 'We thought you should use this in the battle.'

He held out Raya's Amulet of Hiding.

'Why?' Assata asked, eyeing the magic object. She didn't move to take it. 'Raya gave it to you, never me.'

'I think you'll make better use of it this time,' said Og.

The sound of terrified goblin screams emerged from the depths below. The troll had found its first victims, and with any luck was sowing plenty of confusion in the goblin ranks.

'Time to go,' said Krim, and issued her troops the order to attack in a series of violent looking hand gestures.

Assata took the amulet and put it on. She disappeared from view, the magic even suppressing the sound of her movement.

Grim let out a sigh. 'Time for us to go, too.'

✴

Og-Grim-Dog waded through goblinkind. And everywhere they went, they left corpses. Goblins spitted on Og's pike. Goblin heads crushed by Dog's mace. Even goblin chests caved in by a kick from Grim. The rocky terrain of Strong Club ran red with blood and the stink of viscera filled the air.

Dog barked with pleasure.

Even so, more came—committed to the fight, ready to die for their leader. Of course, Og-Grim-Dog would have been quickly overwhelmed if it wasn't for the orc warriors who fought on his side. The orcs found themselves outnumbered. But they were stronger. And not only that, they fought with a rudimentary kind of discipline. A discipline, Grim decided, Krim must have instilled after witnessing humans at war in Kuthenia.

But Grim knew full well that the killing of goblins was merely the appetiser before the main course of this particular battle. And then he came, striding towards Og-Grim-Dog with purpose, and a calm kind of confidence that wasn't for show.

Megrok the Slayer simply believed he was going to kill Og-Grim-Dog.

Megrok only had the one weapon to Og-Grim-Dog's two. It was a huge spiked club, that he could use with one hand or both. Clearly, it was first and foremost a bludgeoning weapon, capable of ending a contest with one well connected blow. But the embedded metal spikes gave Megrok a little more versatility if he so chose: he could stab at opponents, using his formidable strength to pierce through armour.

Even if such a weapon was still not so impressive as a pike and mace combination, Megrok had other advantages. He was taller, with a longer reach. Most importantly, he was far more agile. In full control of his limbs, with only one head, he could outmanoeuvre Grim's more clumsy attempts at movement. He had always got the better of Og-Grim-Dog in the past. That explained his composed demeanour.

This time, of course, it would be a fight to the death. But such trivialities never worried an ogre.

As the two ogres came together, the greenskins around them instinctively gave them space. This would be single combat—a fair fight, that no-one else would intervene in. But the outcome, Grim knew, was likely to swing the wider battle one way or the other.

They circled one another, Og's pike keeping the Slayer at bay. The ogre took his time, studying Grim's movement.

'You've improved,' Megrok noted, his voice a deep rumble. 'But so have I.'

He feinted in one direction, drawing Og's pike towards him, then danced the other way, stepping inside the long weapon. Grim turned to allow Dog to bring his mace in. But somehow, he tripped over his own feet and he lurched forwards, landing heavily on his knees. Pain jarred up his legs, while his upper body pitched forwards. Dog dropped his mace down with all his strength.

The great iron weight landed on Megrok's foot. Grim couldn't help but stare at it, flat and misshapen, as their opponent let out a great roar of agony and anger. Megrok raised his spiked club high, ready to bring it down onto one of the three heads. Perhaps it was the pain; perhaps it was the indecision over which of the three heads to hit first; but he took too long.

Og delivered a perfect thrust. The metal of the pike punched right through the ogre's throat. Megrok's eyes widened in surprise. It looked like he tried to say something—then he clutched the pole of Og's pike with one hand, in an attempt to remove it. Og pushed harder, while Dog swung his mace a second time, taking away Megrok's legs. He fell to the ground with a thud.

Grim got to his feet, peering down at the downed ogre, and the ruin of his throat…and one foot.

'Dead,' Og confirmed, prodding Megrok with the butt of his pike.

'I was assuming,' said Dog, 'that there would be a bit more of a contest there. A bit more back and forth—you know. That it would take a bit longer. It *was* Megrok the Slayer, after all.'

'Yes, well,' said Grim, considering the point. 'Fights don't always work out like that. In real life.'

'Mmm,' said Dog dubiously. 'Whereas, tripping over and hitting them on the foot as the winning move. I suppose *that* happens all the time.'

'There's no need for sarcasm, Dog.'

Whether their defeat of Megrok was unbelievably fortunate or not, Og-Grim-Dog had to take advantage of it. Working with Krim and her orc warriors, they drove the goblins back, until they found themselves entering Gary's underground lair via a wide cave entrance. Ahead, the retreating goblins disappeared into the gloom, perhaps hoping for one final rally.

Krim ordered her troops to move at pace, not allowing the goblins time to reorganise themselves. Grim let the orcs do the work of investigating the dark tunnels and recesses. After all, there was a chance that a draugr troll still roamed the dungeon, and it was preferable that someone else came across it first.

There were some skirmishes along the way—quick, brutal affairs. The orcs dealt with each attack. As they progressed, the dingy, bare dungeon they had entered was replaced by an increasingly well-lit, well-furnished sector. Such signs suggested that they were getting closer to the headquarters of Strong Club— closer, with any luck, to Gary. To revenge.

'This must be it,' said Og.

Finally, they had made it to what looked like the centre of Gary's realm. A huge entranceway into a large chamber gaped before them. Two square pillars flanked the entrance: built for structural support or simply for display, Grim didn't know. From inside the chamber came the flicker of artificial light. It looked very much like the chamber was occupied.

'Advance with care,' Krim told her troops.

Her warriors followed her order and Grim went with them. As he passed into the chamber, he saw a sort of stage at the far end— but made of rock, not wood. A few figures—almost certainly goblins—stood there. In the centre of the chamber was a rather large corpse, surrounded by smaller ones.

So, Grim figured, as the orcs approached the scene—*the draugr troll made it here. Or was it led here?* He noticed they'd peppered the monster with arrows before bringing it down.

Too late, he turned to look up at the walls of the chamber. Twenty feet above the chamber floor was a balcony, reached by several staircases chiselled into the rock wall. The balcony was full of goblins, all armed with bows and arrows. Of course, they were aimed at Og-Grim-Dog and the orcs.

'You made it,' came a familiar voice from the stage. The acoustics of the chamber lifted Gary's words, rolling them around the room like the mighty utterings of a tiny green god. 'In many ways I'm pleased to have had our showdown now, Queen Krim. It would have been quite a nuisance, I expect, having to dig you out of Darkspike. But here you are, generous enough to come to me, with all your soldiers. That error of yours leaves this corner of Gal'azu to me. Thank you.'

'Don't mention it,' Krim spat out. 'You're very fucking welcome, you little twat.'

Gary turned his attention to Og-Grim-Dog. 'Your presence here tells me that Megrok is dead. That is a great shame. I honestly thought you had the sense to come to terms with reality and join us, Og-Grim-Dog. I gave you a chance. I was more than fair. But your chances are all gone now, I'm afraid. Arrghhh!'

It was an odd sight, to see Gary's head pull back, and a line of red blood suddenly appear along his neck, before his body pitched forwards and fell to the floor of the chamber. Quite a shock, really, even for Og-Grim-Dog, who knew it must be the work of Assata. For the goblins, who knew no such thing, Grim understood it must have been very unsettling. It was understandable, he supposed, that they proceeded to make a very great mistake.

Suddenly leaderless, panicky, with an invisible and silent killer on the stage, the goblins on the balcony all did the same thing. Dog would later describe it as a classic example of greenskin groupthink. The goblin archers all fired at the stage. On one level, it worked. For, as well as killing all the other goblins on the stage, Grim quite clearly saw several arrows stop at the same spot, in mid-air, before disappearing. It showed him exactly where Assata was.

On another level, however, the goblins had (quite literally) shot their bolts. Krim and her orcs, seconds away from being fired on from all sides, were suddenly freed. Krim screamed out her orders and her warriors ran, full pelt, for the staircases that led up to the balcony. The goblins were now in quite a fix. Some put new arrows to their bows. Some drew weapons to defend their position as the orcs came rushing up to meet them. But, in general, whatever they did was ineffectual. Krim's orcs, suddenly reprieved, knew that making the balcony as quickly as possible was their path to survival. It wasn't long before goblins were raining down onto the floor of the chamber.

Og-Grim-Dog, however, cared little about all of that. Grim rushed over to the stage and they clambered up at the very spot where Gary had fallen off. It might have been difficult to find Assata, but the barbarian had removed the elven amulet and she was now visible. It only required a brief look for Grim to see that she was done for. Too many arrows had hit too many important parts of her body and there was no healer to rescue her this time.

Og-Grim-Dog knelt by their friend. Assata held the amulet out.

'You can take it back now,' she said, her strong voice suddenly weak. She held her other hand out and Og took it. She looked at them. 'I lived a lot of my life with hate in my heart. I regret that. But I had love, too. And I still think this world is worth saving.' A look of pain passed over her face and she closed her eyes. Her hand dropped to the floor, the amulet slipping from her grasp. 'It's a lot to ask, I know. This world hasn't done you many favours. But you're the only ones left now. Will you try to save it?'

'We'll try,' said Og-Grim-Dog.

They liked to think Assata heard them. Before she died.

✲

'So,' said Grim, his eyes drawn to the spits where the best cuts of goblin were getting roasted. 'You got what you wanted.'

'What was that?' asked Queen Krim doubtfully, her gaze following Grim's. 'Goblin meat ain't my favourite, actually.'

'A kingdom to rule.'

Krim waved her hands to encompass the land about them, then spat on the ground. 'Not quite what I had in mind. There's no-one left to rule over now, is there? Still, I won't quarrel with you. We're the ones who survived the apocalypse. For now, at least. Oh shit.' She raised her voice. 'There's another one!' she called out, as a goblin draugr emerged from the depths of Strong Club, groaning and stumbling its way towards them.

One of her warriors dutifully laid about it with an axe.

'And where are you taking your friend?' Krim asked out of politeness, gesturing at Assata's body, which had been wrapped in a shroud and strapped to Og-Grim-Dog's back.

'We'll bury her with her friend,' said Dog. 'I think she'd have wanted that.'

Krim shrugged with indifference. 'Then what? You know I could find a use for you here. Plenty of draugr still need killing.'

'I think not,' said Grim. 'We'll keep on heading south.'

'Thought as much,' Krim admitted. 'Well. Good luck to you, I suppose.'

Grim began the journey back to Darkspike, leaving the Overlord and her Orc Nation behind.

'South is it, Grim?' Dog asked. 'What do you hope to find there? Not going back to The Swamp, are we?'

'No, not The Swamp. We're going back to Toyer island, to visit with the Guardian of the Portals.'

'Oh. Why are we going back there, Grim?'

'To stop all this from happening, of course.'

POSTMORTEM

The Recorder completed his final flourishes and twirls, then busied himself with drying out the ink on his parchment.

The audience at the Flayed Testicles looked on in a rather uneasy silence. This story hadn't quite been what they were expecting. Their hero had faced his share of danger in his earlier adventures. But there had always been a happy ending. Listening as he recounted the loss of every single one of his friends to a terrifying apocalypse had been a little uncomfortable.

Still, there was something strangely enjoyable about horror stories. Perhaps, mused the regulars and tourists alike, they make you appreciate what you have. As long as the horror happens to other people; somewhere else.

'Well,' said the Recorder finally, 'not entirely what I was expecting to hear. Your account differs, substantially, from others I have heard. In certain particulars.'

'Oh, not this again,' complained the ogre's first head. 'We've told you exactly what happened.'

The Recorder held his hands up. 'I'm not doubting your honesty. Such a traumatic episode in the history of Gal'azu. It's no surprise that people's memories vary.'

'It depends,' said the middle head, 'who you talk to. Some people will say any old nonsense. Whose accounts and memories have you been recording, apart from ours?'

The Recorder raised an indignant eyebrow. 'I don't reveal my sources.'

'What do you mean, you don't reveal your sources?' demanded the third head. 'You've published two books all about us.'

'Yes,' the Recorder agreed. 'But you didn't ask me to protect your identity, did you?'

'Humph. I don't recall you giving us the option.'

'Anyway,' said the Recorder, waving away the complaint. 'We need to discuss the next part of the story.'

'The final part,' corrected the ogre.

The audience at the Testicles gasped and sighed at this revelation. Only one more story to tell?

The Recorder gestured at their fans. 'That's a shame, when we—I mean you—have become so popular.'

'Humph. Some might say it's already gone on long enough.'

'So, this last telling will resolve all the storylines? No loose ends?'

Now it was the ogre's turn to look indignant. 'Of course. What do you take us for? Amateurs?'

The Recorder didn't know what to say to that. 'Then our final meeting needs to be a special occasion. I shall choose the location. We can do better than this dump. No offence intended.'

Everyone looked around at the Testicles. It was hard to argue with that.

END CREDITS

Backstage, the Recorder and the Landlord shared a post-show drink.

'So,' said the Recorder, deciding that he would shamelessly fish for something from the next story. 'You had to go it alone this time. It's going to be a lone wolf type story, eh?'

'No,' said the ogre's middle head. 'We'd lost our friends, that's true. We just needed to get together a new crew.' The ogre paused to think, perhaps wary of revealing too much. 'We found them in the strangest of places.'

✳✳✳

Thanks to everyone who has supported me, including Thomas Edmundson for his help with the plotting for this story and Marcus Nilsson, Adawia Asad & Lisa Maughan for beta reading.

CONNECT WITH THE AUTHOR

Subscribe to Jamie's newsletter to claim your free digital copy of the prequel to The Weapon Takers Saga, *Striking Out*

https://subscribe.jamieedmundson.com/

Website:

jamieedmundson.com

Twitter:

@jamie_edmundson

Og-Grim-Dog: Ogre's End Game

Can Og-Grim-Dog save the world in the fourth novel of the Me Three series.